MOLLY MA

The Sackville Street Caper

'Victorian Dublin is alive – or should that be alive-
alive-oh? Alan Nolan has worked his magic
to reimagine Molly Malone and Bram Stoker
as a young crimefighting duo. A gripping, edge-of-
your-seat caper, filled with big laughs, unforgettable
characters and more twists and turns than the
River Poddle. I adored this book!'

Paul Howard, author of Gordon's Game *and*
Aldrin Adams and the Cheese Nightmares

ALAN NOLAN grew up in Windy Arbour, Dublin and now lives in Bray, Co. Wicklow with his wife and three children. Alan is the author and illustrator of *Fintan's Fifteen*, *Conor's Caveman* and the *Sam Hannigan* series, and is the illustrator of *Animal Crackers: Fantastic Facts About Your Favourite Animals*, written by Sarah Webb. Alan runs illustration and writing workshops for children, and you may see him lugging his drawing board and pencils around your school or local library.

www.alannolan.ie

Twitter: @AlNolan

Instagram: @alannolan_author

MOLLY MALONE & BRAM STOKER IN

The Sackville Street Caper

ALAN NOLAN

THE O'BRIEN PRESS
DUBLIN

This edition first published 2022 by
The O'Brien Press Ltd,
12 Terenure Road East, Rathgar,
Dublin 6, D06 HD27, Ireland.
Tel: +353 1 4923333; Fax: +353 1 4922777
E-mail: books@obrien.ie
Website: obrien.ie
The O'Brien Press is a member of Publishing Ireland

ISBN: 978-1-78849-318-5
Text © copyright Alan Nolan, 2022
The moral rights of the author have been asserted
Copyright for typesetting, layout, editing, design
© The O'Brien Press Ltd
Layout and design by Emma Byrne
Cover illustration by Shane Cluskey
Internal illustration p223 by Shane Cluskey
Map and internal chapter header illustrations by Alan Nolan
Author photograph p2 by Sam Nolan

8 7 6 5 4 3 2 1
22 24 25 23

Printed in the UK by Clays Ltd, St Ives plc.
The paper in this book is produced using pulp from managed forests.

Molly Malone and Bram Stoker in The Sackville Street Caper
receives financial assistance from the Arts Council

DEDICATION
For Don

TABLE OF CONTENTS

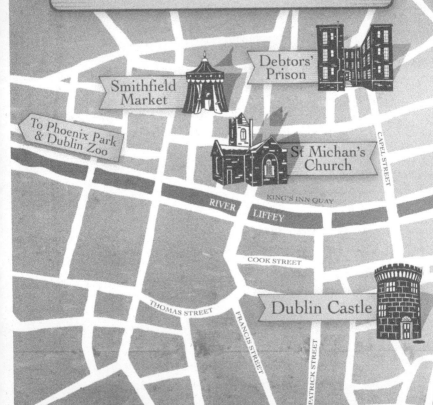

Messrs Hardiman
& Braithwaite's

Patented Map
of Dublin City
1858
Revised Edition

Debtors'
Prison

Smithfield
Market

To Phoenix Park
& Dublin Zoo

St Michan's
Church

CAPEL STREET

KING'S INN QUAY

RIVER LIFFEY

COOK STREET

THOMAS STREET

FRANCIS STREET

Dublin Castle

PATRICK STREET

MUD ISLAND

Molly's Shack

NEWCOMEN BRIDGE

To Clontarf & Howth

DORSET STREET

The Rotunda Round Room

GT BRITAIN ST

SACKVILLE STREET

GARDINER STREET

TALBOT ST.

Nelson's Pillar

HENRY STREET

ABBEY STREET

NORTH WALL

RIVER LIFFEY

GEORGE'S QUAY

HA'PENNY BRIDGE

CARLISLE BRIDGE

ENTRANCE TO RIVER PODDLE

GT BRUNSWICK STREET

DAME STREET

TRINITY COLLEGE

EXCHEQUER STREET

NASSAU STREET

GRAFTON ST

DAWSON STREET

KILDARE STREET

MERRION SQUARE

ST STEPHEN'S GREEN

A Short List of Characters Contained Within, Provided by the Most Considerate Author for Your Instruction and Delight:

Bram Stoker

The future author of *Dracula*, eleven years of age, yearns for adventure and to have stories to tell.

Molly Malone

Eleven years of age, accomplished sneak thief and part-time fishmonger.

Shep, Rose, Billy the Pan, Calico Tom, aka The Sackville Street Spooks

Molly's gang, to whom she is part sergeant major, part mother hen.

Count Vladimir Grof–Constantin de Lugosi, Knight–Indigent of Transylvania

A down-at-heel (yet spookily Gothic) Transylvanian count, who plans to rob the Irish Crown Jewels to pay off the numerous gambling debts he has accrued across Europe.

Messrs Bounderby & Caddsworth

The Count's short, bumbling, slightly dim-witted sidekicks; they are almost identical in appearance, but for the fact that one of the villains has a moustache and no beard, while the other miscreant has a beard and no moustache.

Madame Florence

A fortune teller at Smithfield Market, variously known as the Seer of the What-Is-To-Come, the One Who Knows All, the Seventh Daughter of a Seventh Daughter, and the White Witch of Westmoreland Street.

Wild Bert Florence

A semi-retired Wild West trick-rider from 'this side of the Mississippi', USA, and Madame Flo's husband.

Abraham Stoker

Bram's strait-laced civil servant father, and Keeper of the Crown Jewels at Dublin Castle.

ADVENTURE AWAITS!

Bram lit the candle on his bedside table and tall, creepy shadows instantly began to dance around the dormitory walls. Outside, a harsh gust of night wind blew through the branches of a tree, causing its bony twig fingers to tap and scrape against the windowpane.

As usual, Bram was the last boy awake in the dormitory. He wasn't at all worried that the wind, or the scraping twigs, or the dim candlelight would wake up the other boys in the room as they slept, row by row, in their cots – if they could manage to sleep through Nesbitt's incessant snoring, they could sleep though anything!

He stared thoughtfully at the shadows as he chewed his pencil. *That one fluttering around the gas lamp fitting looks like a bat*, he thought, *and this one crouching beside the wardrobe looks like an evil witch about to pounce*! He smiled nervously, thinking about his plan for the next day, the plan he had mapped out in his mind for so many weeks. He opened his leather-bound diary and began to write.

The Diary of Master Abraham Stoker
22nd of August 1858
Howth, County Dublin

Well, Dearest Diary,

The decision is made; this shall be my last night in Mrs Harker's Academy, and I find that now my mind is finally set on escape, my heart is bursting with both anticipation and relief.

I should like to rise from my bed and shout for joy, to open up the window and cry HALLOOO! into the cool night air, but I fear I may wake the other boys in the dorm.

But although I shall miss everybody (even Mrs Harker), I find the Academy so *boring*! I am intent on becoming a writer, but *how* am I to be a writer if I attend an Academy where *nothing ever happens*?

So, it is time to move on. Even if only for a few days.

Next month I am to start my senior school education in the Reverend Wood's School – another famously dreary establishment – but before that, I intend to embark on AN ADVENTURE.

Tomorrow, while Mrs Harker and the boys are on the walking trip to Howth Harbour, will be the perfect time to make my escape.

I shall walk the dusty road to Sutton Cross, then through Bayside and on along the coast path. I shall hurry through Clontarf for fear Mama or, even worse, Papa should spy me on my journey. I may even flag down a passing carriage or cart – I have heard some of the boys in the dorm refer to the practice as 'cart-cadging' — and ask the driver if I may accompany him into Dublin.

For it is there in Dublin City that I shall become a writer. All the action and excitement and incidents of Ireland occur in the big city. I shall experience REAL LIFE there, I shall see stories unfold before my eyes; in short, I shall have something to write about!

But don't you worry, Dearest Diary — I shan't leave you behind.

Wheresoever I will go, you shall be by my side (or at least, in my knapsack).

So, until the morrow, D.D. — ADVENTURE awaits!

Bram

CHAPTER I

SCHOOL'S OUT!

IN WHICH YOUNG MASTER BRAM STOKER SLIPS AWAY FROM
SCHOOL TO PURSUE A LIFE OF ADVENTURE!

Bram placed his pencil inside the pages of his
diary and, reaching down, tucked the small,
leather-bound book into his knapsack and quietly
shoved it under his bed beside his chamber pot.

He looked around at the other boys in the dorm,
or at least, the ones he could see by the dim light
of his candle. He couldn't see Nesbitt, but he knew

he was there by the droning snore that bounced off the wooden panels of the room. He smiled as he remembered how Cooky had stitched a pocket into the back of Nesbitt's pyjamas, right between the shoulder blades, in an effort to stop him snoring.

'Pop a walnut into the pocket, dear,' she told him. 'That way, every time you turn on your back and start snoring, the walnut will dig into you and make you tip over onto your side again.'

This plan worked for a couple of noise-free nights, but unfortunately Cooky's scheme had two fatal flaws – one was that Nesbitt loved to eat walnuts; the other was that Nesbitt's parents had kindly gifted him a nutcracker the previous Christmas. He went through almost a shilling's worth before Cooky admitted defeat.

Bram licked his thumb and forefinger and extinguished the candle. He closed his eyes and made an inventory in his head. Shoes. Short trousers. Underwear. An old jacket, not too fancy. Coin purse. All under the spare blanket at the end of his bed. In the morning he would help himself to some bread and cheese from the kitchen as he left. And some string.

Must remember some string. You never know when you will need string. He reached down in the darkness and felt for his knapsack. Still there. Right beside the chamber pot. *Oh dear.* Maybe he was nervous about tomorrow's planned escape, but he decided he'd better use the chamber pot again.

* * *

The next morning Cooky sounded the gong at seven o'clock sharp, as she did every morning, apart from Sundays, when she sounded it at seven thirty. Nesbitt's job was to open the curtains, and he shuffled sleepily over to the window to fulfil this duty. The day was fresh and bright, and the sun was shining. *Perfect*, thought Bram.

As the boys lined up to wash at the two basins of cold water, Bram once again checked his running-away clothes and peeked under his bed to make sure his knapsack was still there.

Once washed, the boys all dressed in their school uniform of short trousers, navy blue knee socks, white wing-collared shirt, black bow tie and crested navy jacket. As soon as Bram and Nesbitt had helped some of the younger boys tie their bow ties – Bram always felt they could be frightfully fiddly for little fingers – the boys lined up again at the door, paced out onto the landing and descended the wide mahogany staircase, all in unison, like a platoon of miniature soldiers marching to the battlefield. Halfway down, Bram faked a sneeze, jerking his body violently.

'I say,' said Nesbitt, taking him by the elbow, 'are you all right, old boy?'

Bram straightened up, 'Tickety-boo, old chap, never better.'

After breakfast the boys gathered in the assembly room where Mrs Harker greeted them with the same closed-mouthed smile that greeted them every morning, a smile that, though wide, never quite seemed to reach her eyes. She was a tall, thin woman with a severe hairstyle that was pulled back so tightly that it stretched the skin of her face. This was topped with one enormous bun of jet-black hair that sat on the top of her head. Bram thought that the bun looked like a round, corpulent crow, asleep up there with its own head tucked under its wing. This made him smile, but his smile, unlike Mrs Harker's, reached his eyes.

Mrs Harker coughed sharply to silence the already quiet room and the boys quickly snapped to attention. She brushed the front of her raven-black dress and placed a pair of *pince-nez* spectacles on the bridge of her hooked nose. Bram smiled to himself again; she really *did* look like a bird.

'Good morning, boys,' shrilled Mrs Harker in her twittery voice. 'Are we all excited for our little walking trip?' She began to organise the boys into a very straight, military-style line, 'It's a pity you won't be joining us, Master Stoker,' she said, 'but perhaps a day of solitary study and quiet contemplation will be beneficial for your cold, eh?'

Mrs Harker patted Bram's head and smiled with the bottom half of her face. 'Rest, Master Stoker, plenty of rest,' she trilled, and led the boys out the ornate wooden front door, crunching down the gravel path towards the village, with a cheerfully saluting Nesbitt bringing up the rear.

Bram closed the door and bolted up the stairs to the dorm. He quickly changed into his travel things and bundled his school clothes under the bed covers, doing his best to make it look like he himself was lying asleep in the bed. He pulled the heavy curtain closed to add to the illusion. He grabbed his knapsack and quickly used the chamber pot again. *Gosh*, he thought, *I am nervous.*

He crept quietly down the stairs and slithered past the dining room where good old Cooky was clearing up. Passing through the kitchen, he wrapped half a loaf of fresh white bread and a large lump of pale orange cheese in a cloth and put them in his knapsack.

Then, looking around to make sure Cooky wasn't watching, he quietly opened the kitchen door and stepped out into the sunshine.

CHAPTER 2

MEET MOLLY

IN WHICH CHAMPION SNEAK THIEF MOLLY MALONE PREPARES HER
SPOOKS FOR A HARD DAY'S HAUNTING.

'Take that saucepan off your head.'

'No.'

'Take it off.'

'No!'

Molly took a step towards Billy the Pan. Billy the
Pan took a step backwards.

'Why do you wear that saucepan anyways, Billy?'

asked Shep.

'Me da says I need a trade,' said Billy, not taking his eyes off Molly.

'A trade? Your da's a beggarman!' laughed Shep.

'And so was me granda, and so was me granda's da. It's not easy to make a livin' as a beggarman now-adays. Dublin's full of beggarmen. Me da says you need to be able to stand out. So, I wear a saucepan on me head.' Billy knocked his knuckles on the battered side of the pan. It sounded hollow.

'Not today,' said Molly, balling her fingers into fists. 'We are going bobbing today. And bobbers who don't want to get caught by the constables don't try to stand out from the crowd.' Molly's eyebrows furrowed and she jutted out her freckle-covered chin. 'Take it off. Now.'

Billy knew that look. He took the saucepan off.

'Right,' said Molly, 'line up and let's have a look at you.' She stuck her two thumbs into the ragged, once-white pinafore she wore over her faded blue dress and inspected her crew like a particularly picky Dragoon Guard drill sergeant. In all her years she had never seen a sorrier-looking bunch.

Billy was lanky, had the beginnings of a moustache and could have passed for a servant, *(perhaps a footman?)* if his clothes were less ragged and he wasn't carrying that stupid saucepan. Shep was around eight or nine – he didn't know when his birthday was – with tight, curly black hair and a constantly dribbling nose. Rose was ten, with red hair just like Molly; she wore a blue dress, stolen from a washing line in Bride Street, so she could look even more like her idol. Calico Tom was the smallest of the gang, an orphan with wavy blonde hair and a cherubic baby face who looked much younger than his six years – he could almost pass for a toddler. *He'll be a stunner when he's older,* thought Molly, *but his arms are too little to reach into the Qualitys' pockets – he will have to be the lookout. Or maybe the distraction?*

Lastly, of course, there was Her Majesty: a knee-high mutt with curly brown fur, big floppy ears, and a long, lolling tongue. She was always slightly smelly, but in Molly's opinion gave the best cuddles in Dublin.

'All right,' said Molly, 'here's the plan.'

She stood and scratched her freckly chin for several

long seconds, then she bent down and scratched Her Majesty's chin too.

'It's the "Lost Baby" caper again,' declared Molly, standing up, 'We go to Sackville Street as a gang, hiding Calico Tom from view. When we get to the Pillar, we drop the "baby" and walk away. Calico, how's your wailing?'

'I can wail like a mountain goat, Mol,' said the tiny boy in an unexpectedly deep voice. 'No bother at all.'

'Grand,' said Molly, 'Next, Tom wails that he's lost his mammy. The Quality gathers to see what's wrong with him ... and then we do our magic tricks.'

'Our magic tricks?' asked Rose, who was new to the game.

'Making wallets, pocketbooks and silk handker-chiefs disappear, of course,' replied Molly.

'Right, there's money to be made – Spooks, let's go a-hauntin'!'

CHAPTER 3

DUBLIN'S FAIR CITY

IN WHICH BRAM ARRIVES IN DUBLIN CITY, IS PILFERED BY
PICKPOCKETS, AND ALMOST SPLITS HIS KIPPER.

The cart began to rattle noisily as the iron wheels clattered over cobblestones. The big sow stirred in her sleep and a few of her piglets squealed in alarm. 'Sssssshhhhh,' said Bram and patted the sleeping pig. 'I think we're arriving in the big city at last!' He pulled himself up into a sitting position, brushed down his jacket and picked

25

straw out of his hair.

'Ah, young master,' said the cart's driver, pulling back on the reins and halting the huge, brown dray horse that hauled the wooden wagon, 'here we are now in Elephant Lane. The Pro-Cathedral's on your right and Sackville Street is dead ahead. You couldn't be more in the centre of Dublin if you wanted to.' He threw his head back and laughed, revealing a total of three brownish teeth. 'Thanks for taking care of Arabella and the little ones.'

'Good luck at the market,' shouted Bram as he jumped down off the back of the cart, 'and thanks again for the lift!' He would remember his journey into Dublin with Arabella the pig for a very long time. *At the very least*, he thought, *I shall smell like Arabella the pig for a very long time …*

The driver waved and gave the horse's backside a gentle pat of his bamboo switch, and the wagon pulled off slowly and creakily in the direction of Smithfield Market. Bram looked around in wonder and excitement. *Dublin at last!* he thought, *what adventures shall I have here?* He walked past the imposing cathedral and, emerging from the shadows of Elephant Lane, stepped out onto Sackville Street, the grandest and busiest thoroughfare in the whole of Ireland. *Yes, THIS is where I shall become a writer!*

He was instantly surrounded by people, bustle and noise. And all the wonderful smells! Women with baskets of delicious-smelling bread; men with wicker hampers of sweet strawberries, ripe raspberries and fresh fruit; and fishmongers with barrows of shellfish, haddock and prawns that smelt of, well ... fish. All were calling out their wares for sale in loud, sing-song voices.

Across the wide street (the widest main street in Europe according to Mrs Harker), Bram could see the six stone columns of the Post Office, and in front of that, Nelson's Pillar, erected in honour of Admiral Horatio Nelson, Britain's great naval hero. He remembered his papa calling the huge stone pillar *Dublin's Glory* when they had passed by it in a cab on their way to the Theatre Royal the previous Christmas. Bram's old nanny back at his childhood home in Clontarf's leafy Marino Crescent had another name for the Pillar: she called it *Horatio's Peg Leg*. 'There's a viewing platform near the top of the peg, should you have a head for heights,' his nanny had told him when he was small. 'The views over the city are a sight to see!'

Bram skipped nimbly through the parade of horse-drawn carts and hansom cabs to the centre of the street where gentlemen dressed in fine red and blue jackets and shiny top hats, and ladies in long, ornate, pastel-coloured dresses strolled along together, taking the morning air.

He was staring up at the top of the Pillar, where Nelson's stone sword arm was just visible above the railings of the viewing platform, when his attention was caught by a commotion at the other side of the base. A group of well-to-do ladies and gentlemen had gathered around what looked like a crying toddler. The child was small and wore a shabby red jacket with a grubby lace collar. On his bottom half he wore a huge calico cloth nappy, from which emerged two chubby bare legs. The toddler was sitting in the dust, beating the ground with his little arms and wailing loudly for his mother.

'Maaaaaaaaaammmmaaaaaaaaa!' he cried, 'I want my muh-muh-muh-muh-Maaaaaaaaaammmaaaaaaaaa!'

'Oh, Maurice,' Bram heard a well-dressed lady say to her top-hatted companion, 'you simply must summon a constable. A child that small should not be out here alone without his mother; he may be trampled by a horse or a tradesman!'

Bram did not think the child was as alone as he seemed to be, however. Several bigger children, all dressed in clothes just as shabby as the baby's jacket, were circling quietly behind the crowd of adult onlookers – a tall boy of around twelve years, holding a scruffy dog on a string; a smaller, brown-skinned boy with a runny nose; and at least two red-haired girls. As Bram watched these children, he could see them gently push the grown-ups apart, pretending to be looking for a better view of the lost child, and at the same time silently slipping their small hands into the gentlemen's pockets and removing bank notes and handkerchiefs. One of the red-haired girls even used a small scissors to cut the ribbon on a lady's reticule handbag, magically causing the small bag to disappear into the folds of her faded blue dress. None of the grown-ups noticed what they were doing.

Bram smiled. He had read about these kinds of

wild children in the newspapers back at Mrs Harker's Academy – 'pickpockets' they were called, or, quite fittingly considering the circumstances, 'cut-purses'. *Well*, he thought amiably, *these children have to eat too. And they do seem very skilled in what they–*

Suddenly he felt a movement at his left arm, light as a summer breeze, and the small weight that had burdened him since he left the Academy that morning lessened slightly. He patted the strap of the knapsack on his shoulder and found himself patting only the fabric of his jacket. *My diary*, he thought. 'My diary!' he cried. 'Those children have stolen my diary!'

With that, the 'baby' in the middle of the onlookers jumped to his chubby feet, hoisted up his nappy and ran like a demon straight across the street, deftly avoiding cabs and carts as he darted into the relative shade of Henry Street. He was followed by an equally fast-moving blur with black hair. The rest of the wild children had disappeared, as if by magic.

All around Bram gentlemen and ladies were patting their own now-empty pockets and staring disbelievingly at ribbons in their hands that were no longer attached to reticules. A general cry went up of 'Thief!' but it was too late – the adults had no idea who or what had taken their goods, or to where the phantom perpetrators had suddenly vanished.

Bram did though! He casually walked across Sackville Street and, on reaching Henry Street, broke into a run. *They can keep the knapsack,* he thought, *but I must, MUST, have my diary back!*

Henry Street was quieter than the main thoroughfare, with a few traders and shopkeepers fussing about their window displays. There were some beggars ambling along too, but Bram couldn't see anyone who looked like they were actually *fleeing*.

By chance, he glanced to his right and saw, in the darkness of a laneway, the silhouettes of two children, one small and the other even smaller, laughing and clapping each other on the back. Between them they held open a canvas knapsack and were perusing the contents. Bram made for the mouth of the laneway and, reaching it, said, as amiably as he could, 'Hello chaps. I say, I was wondering if I could please have my diary from that knapsack?'

The two children looked up in fright, glanced at each other for a moment, and then took off at speed down the laneway. *Oh dear*, thought Bram. *They may be quick on their toes, but I dare say I may be a touch faster.*

Bram was an enthusiastic sporting star at Mrs Harker's Academy, where he had earned a reputation for his speed and agility and could easily outpace any boy on either the school rugby or cricket team. He was sure he could out-run these young ruffians!

The laneway took a sudden left and then a right turn, and Bram skidded around these corners, his feet sliding on the smooth cobblestones. He could see the two boys taking another sharp left ahead when he heard a sudden call from somewhere far above, 'HA-LOOOWW, BE-LOOOWW!'

He felt a shoulder barge into him, knocking him sideways, just out of the course of the yellow contents of a chamber pot which splashed harmlessly, if stinkily, onto the cobbles beside him. *Thank goodness! A close call!*

The barging shoulder belonged to a silent lightning bolt with red hair, which had shot past him, never breaking her stride, and had already rounded the corner. Bram looked up at the window from whence the contents of the chamber pot came and shook his head. *Dublin,* he thought, *the sights and smells …*

Resuming the chase, Bram quickly took the next left and found himself on Moore Street. The street was jam-packed with carts, barrows, beggars and street sellers, selling everything from antiques and clothes to flowers, fish, meat and vegetables. He would never find those children amongst this throng of people; his diary was lost for sure.

Just then, Bram spotted something. Lying discarded amongst the debris on the rubbish-strewn ground was a familiar-looking large calico cloth nappy. Reaching it, he spied a head of jet-black curly hair quietly bobbing behind a cart. 'Hey,' shouted Bram, 'Hello! I just want to talk!' The head ducked down and dashed, and Bram followed it through the crowd. The black-haired boy had the smaller child by the hand, and they sped into another lane with Bram in hot pursuit.

As he rounded the corner into the lane, Bram felt his shoes slip on the cobbles as they had before, but this time they kept slipping. The cobbles in this laneway weren't just worn smooth with age, they were slimy and slick, as if they were coated in some sort of thick oil, and once Bram started to skid, he found he couldn't stop. He put his arms out wide to balance himself, desperately trying to keep his feet as he slipped sideways, but his legs connected with the low side of a long wooden container and he flipped into it, twisting himself onto his side as he fell and bracing himself for a hard landing.

Instead, he was most surprised to find that the landing was soft. Very soft, in fact. And extremely squishy. Not to mention exceedingly smelly. He sat up and looked at his two hands. Both were dripping with thick red and green slime. *FISH GUTS!* The container was full of smelly, stinking, disgusting fish guts – fish heads, fish kidneys, fish livers, rotten fish tails, rotten fins and rotten tentacles. An empty oyster shell sat in Bram's lap, and in the centre of the shell, where a pearl might be, sat a rancid, cloudy fish eyeball. It seemed to be glaring up at him.

Bram choked. He wanted to take a deep breath, but knew if he did, Cooky's excellent breakfast would join the mess of festering fish parts he was now sitting in.

He stood up in the cold, disgusting fish soup, a charmless chowder that came to nearly the top of his knee stockings, and with his hand on the side of the slimy wooden bay for balance, he stepped gingerly out.

To his surprise, the black-haired boy and the toddler were standing a little down the laneway, staring at him with wrinkled faces. The taller boy was holding Bram's knapsack, while the smaller one was holding up a pair of saggy shorts with one hand; both were waving their free hand under their noses to waft away the stench of the rotten fish.

Bram wiped the fish goo off his face with his filthy jacket sleeve and blinked at them. As one, the two rogues quickly turned and ran. *Not again*, thought Bram. 'Wait!' he shouted, and stumbled after them, slipping on the cobbles as he went.

But this time he didn't have to stumble for long. The end of the lane was a dead end, a *cul-de-sac* as Mrs Harker would say – a tall, flat wall with overflowing tin rubbish bins lined up in front of it. The two young thieves had nowhere to go and, pulling up with a screech, they spun around to face their dogged pursuer.

Bram stopped and panted. Despite his undoubted sporting prowess, he was worn out from running, he was down one diary, and, worst of all, he was covered in fish guts and smelled like three-week-old, lukewarm vomit. He picked a fish tail from his hair, flicked it to the ground and glared at the two boys. 'All right, enough's enough,' he said. 'Hand over my diary and we'll say no mo–'

KLLANNGGGG!!!!

Bram's eyes met each other at the top of his nose, and he crumpled onto the cobblestones with a stinky, fishy squelch.

'Billy,' said Molly, emerging from behind the bins, 'why'd you have to hit him so hard? You nearly split his kipper!'

'Sorry, Molly,' mumbled Billy the Pan. 'I only got this new saucepan last week – I grew out of me last one – an' I didn't know how hard it was.'

'Ah, look at him,' said Rose, standing over Bram's stupefied body. 'Poor chicken, he's out cold.' She comforted Her Majesty, who was whimpering and pulling back on her rope to get further away from the dreadful smell.

'Well, we can't leave him here in the street,' said Molly. 'The snatchers will sell him to the student doctors in Trinity for body parts. We'll have to bring him with us.'

Sighing, Billy and Shep reluctantly grabbed the inert, fish-gut-stinking body of Bram Stoker under the armpits, and, with Molly, Rose and Calico Tom in tow, they carried him off to Mud Island.

NOTICE:

○

TO WHOM IT MAY CONCERN:

MISSING CHILD

○

**IT IS WITH GREAT CONSTERNATION
THAT WE MUST ANNOUNCE THAT
A CHILD IS MISSING**

ABRAHAM OR BRAM, COMING FROM
A GOOD FAMILY IN CLONTARF,
IS ELEVEN YEARS, QUITE TALL, WITH
A ROUNDED FACE AND A FAIR COMPLEXION

A **REWARD** IS OFFERED FOR THE
SAFE RETURN OF THIS CHILD

APPLY TO MR A. STOKER, ESQ.,
THE CRESCENT, CLONTARF
OR LATELY AT TAVISTOCK TOWER,
DUBLIN CASTLE

○

GOD SAVE THE QUEEN!

CHAPTER 4

STUCK IN THE MUD (ISLAND)

IN WHICH BRAM FINDS OUT THAT NOT ALL SPOOKS ARE SCARY.

What woke Bram up was the searing pain in his head. What made him wish he was still unconscious was the smell.

'What IS that STENCH?' he splurted through gritted teeth, his hand involuntarily going to his nose, 'Urrrghhhh!' He staggered to his feet, holding onto the wall as he got up. It felt like rough, untreated wood – was he in someone's gardening shed?

'That smell is fish guts, fish heads, rotten cockles and, oh yes, rotten mussels,' said a voice to his left, 'You fell into a fishmonger's pit. Like an eejit.'

If Bram had been able to open his eyes, he could have seen who was speaking, but his face was just too scrunched up by the truly abominable whiff. 'I … the *smell* … I have to wash,' he said, his eyes still tightly shut. 'May I use the washbasin, please, if you have one?'

'Of course, sir! The washbasin is through the first door on your right,' said the voice chirpily. Bram felt a hand guide him by the elbow and heard the creak of a door opening. He felt cold, fresh air. *Strange*, he thought. He put his foot forward and stepped through the door and out into absolute nothingness, his body toppling forward head-first for a few seconds … and then SSPPLASSSHHHHing into freezing, green water. He tumbled over in the water and, despite the bone-chilling cold, reflexively started pushing downwards with his arms and kicking his feet. His head broke the surface and, wiping the brackish water from his eyes, he looked up to see a red-haired girl staring down at him and laughing.

She wore a shabby, faded blue dress and was slapping her knees with mirth. Bram had never seen anyone laugh like that before. When he told a joke at school the most he ever received in return was a polite smile and a nod. He must have done something very funny indeed to make this strange girl laugh so hard. Tears began to stream down her face.

'I'm so glad I amuse you,' said Bram, treading water, 'Perhaps you could help me up?'

Still giggling, the girl reached down and grabbed Bram's outstretched hand. 'It's not you falling that I'm laughin' at,' said the girl as she helped Bram to scramble up the slippery, slime-covered side of the canal. 'It's the fact that you thought that our rotten old shack had an indoor washroom! The only place we wash ourselves is in the Royal Canal, like nature intended.'

'Welcome to Mud Island,' said the girl, wiping tears from her green eyes. 'I'm Molly. Molly Malone.'

'Bram Stoker,' said Bram, heaving himself up to sit in the doorway that opened right onto the canal side. 'Well, Abraham is my proper name – that's what Mama and Papa call me; my friends call me Bram. I suppose I'm pleased to meet you?' He leant forward and peered up and down the canal. *Where was he?*

'You're at the lock at Newcomen Bridge,' said Molly, reading his puzzled expression. 'Our hut here is an old storage shed attached to the lock-keeper's cottage. The door here used to be used for loading stuff onto barges.' She hauled Bram to his feet and pulled him inside the shack. 'But it's our place now, our little hidey-hole.'

Bram's eyes took a moment to adjust to the candlelight inside. The walls of the hut were indeed rough wood, but nearly every inch of the walls was covered with bunches of hanging handkerchiefs, silk scarves, waistcoats, morning coats, lace reticules and fine leather money purses. The floor was covered in wooden crates filled with all sorts of items that had no business at all being in a ramshackle hut. There was a crate of chisels, planes and other woodworking tools, another crate containing fountain pens and ink pots, and another filled with children's colourfully painted tin toys. There were small crates of dainty leather gloves, a wooden box packed full of glass perfume bottles, and another overflowing with pink-

and cream-coloured soaps. Against one wall rested a large fabric handbag; its leather handle had a card label attached that read 'COSTUME JEWELLERY – WORTHLESS.' Amongst the crates and boxes there were five bundles of straw bedding and rough blankets, and in the centre of the hut was a table with five chairs. Sitting on the chairs counting coins and large white bank notes were four children, two of whom looked very familiar to Bram. The taller of the two, a boy with jet-black, curly hair looked up from a red, leather-bound book.

'My diary!' shouted Bram, outraged.

'Oh, hold your whisht,' said Molly beside him, 'Don't worry about that young fella finding out all your secrets – he can't read.' She nodded to Shep, 'Give it back to the young gentleman, Shep.'

Shep closed the diary and tossed it to Bram. Bram caught it and hugged it to his chest, realised his chest was wet and, looking around for somewhere dry to put it, placed it gently on top of a box full of ornate teapots. A girl with red hair, who bore a striking resemblance to the girl who had introduced her-self as Molly, stood from the table and passed him a towel, which he took gratefully; it was early evening, the sun was going down and it was beginning to get cold.

'That's Rose,' said Molly, pointing to her doppelganger. Now Bram looked at them both together he could see that they only looked superficially the same, with similar dresses and hair. Their faces were quite different; Molly had more freckles and Rose had a pointier nose. Rose looked a little younger than Molly too. 'You've met Shep, of course,' Molly continued, 'and the little dote in the corner is Calico Tom.'

'I told ya, Mol,' said Calico in his surprisingly deep voice, 'stop callin' me a dote.'

Molly winked at him, 'Billy the Pan is the fella that clonked your crown, but he's got a family; he's gone home for his dinner.'

'He's got a family?' asked Bram. 'Does that mean that you don't have one? That you live here alone? With no adults? How exciting!'

'We DO have a family!' exclaimed Rose fiercely, standing up and jutting out her chin in a most Molly-like manner. 'We have each other!'

Bram's eyes widened and he took a step back, 'Oh! I apologise! I didn't mean to cause any offence, that would be the last thing—'

'No offence taken,' said Molly, smiling, 'It's us that owe *you* an apology, as it happens. You see, we thought you were Quality – you know, one of the rich people – but it seems you only had a few loose coins, a ball of string and a book in your knapsack.'

'That book is my Diary, and is the most important thing to me,' said Bram, picking his diary off the crate of teapots and cradling it defensively. 'It's where I capture my thoughts and feelings – this Diary is my best friend and my dearest confidant.'

'If his best friend is a book, he MUST be Quality, Mol,' said Shep. 'Only a high-falutin' young master jellyspoon would claim that his best friend is a book!'

'I believe that if one is to be a writer,' said Bram defensively, 'one's best friends *should* be books. That is why I came to the city in the first place – to escape my school, to have adventures and to write about them in my diary – so that one day I should have enough experiences, enough excitement and have lived enough life to be able to write books!' He felt something wet and warm, sloppily tickling his hand, and looked down. A knee-high dog of indeterminate breed with great furry, floppy ears stared back at him, its huge brown eyes shining.

'And that's Her Majesty,' said Molly. Her Majesty seemed to give Bram a wide, friendly smile and began licking his hand again. 'I think she likes you,' said Molly, ruffling Her Majesty's furry head, 'Either that or she thinks you're tasty.'

'Her Majesty?' asked Bram. He had never heard such a name for a dog, a name so cheekily disrespectful to the great Victoria, Queen of the United Kingdom of Great Britain and Ireland. Bram was quite sure none of the boys in his school would ever dare give a dog such an impudent name. He *loved* it. He smiled, and petted Her Majesty's head too. 'Well, I seem to have gotten the Royal Seal of Approval!'

'Hey, what's-yer-name,' said Rose, 'you can read, can't ya?' Bram looked up and nodded. 'Me and Shep will get the dinner, and you can read us a story afterwards.'

With the mention of dinner, Bram's mouth started to water. It seemed like *years* since he had eaten breakfast at Mrs Harker's Academy, and the thought of Cooky's porridge with sultanas and apple slices, rashers of finest bacon and toasted home-made soda bread made him even hungrier. 'That sounds like a deal,' he said. 'What's for dinner?' Bram looked around the hut; he couldn't see a stove, or even a fireplace where the gang might fry up some meat or boil vegetables in a pot.

'Mud Island surprise!' smiled Rose, pulling some of the scarves and handkerchiefs out of their loosely packed bundles on the walls. 'We go from house to house ...'

'Or hut to hut,' interjected Shep.

'Or hut to hut,' continued Rose, looking sharply at the smaller boy, but giving him a playful punch on the arm, 'and swap some of our prizes for whatever food they are cooking.'

'It's usually potatoes,' said Shep, 'but sometimes we get cabbage or carrots or mashed turnip.'

Rose sighed and licked her lips, 'Mmmmmmm ... Mashed turnip ...'

Calico Tom grabbed a couple of handkerchiefs and took Rose by the hand. 'Sometimes we even get some meat!' he said, smiling broadly.

'Choose a story to read, you,' said Rose, pointing at a wooden box of assorted books and winking at Bram, 'We'll be back soon!' They left by the front door – the one that *didn't* open onto the canal.

Molly plonked herself down on a crate of stuffed toy animals, and Her Majesty curled up at her feet. She sat still and silent for a long moment. 'We're not really thieves, you know,' she said quietly.

Bram raised his eyebrows. *Yes, they ARE thieves*, he thought.

'Well, yes, we *are* thieves,' said Molly, 'but we don't steal to get rich; we only steal so we can eat. And to live as free as we please. Mind you, sometimes living free means going hungry; when nobody wants what we have to trade, well, then we just don't eat.'

Bram didn't know how to respond to that – the cupboards at 15 Marino Crescent and at Mrs Harker's Academy were always brimming with food. 'So, you don't go to school?' he asked, taking books out of the wooden box and reading their titles, 'or church?' Molly shook her head. 'And no parents looking in? Well,' Bram corrected himself, 'that other chap had parents, of course, Willy the Pot.'

'Billy the Pan!' laughed Molly. 'We all *had* families; Shep, Rose, Calico, even Her Majesty here had a mam and dad. We all just got *lost* along the way. I had a mam and dad meself, fishmongers they were.'

'What happened to them?' asked Bram in a low voice.

'Oh, they died,' said Molly, 'a long time ago. In the Workhouse.'

'I'm so sorry,' said Bram. 'I didn't mean to pry. I can't imagine what it would be like to have no family.' He thought of his own mama and papa; did they know he had left the Academy without permission? Were they looking for him?

'But Rose is right. We have a family; *this* is our family!' said Molly firmly, making Her Majesty look sleepily up at her from her spot on the floor. 'Right here – me, Billy, Rose, Shep and Calico.' The dog barked, making both Molly and Bram laugh. 'And Her Majesty too.'

'We call ourselves the Sackville Street Spooks, 'cause we glide like ghosts through the Quality,' said Molly, 'Rich people don't bother looking at the poor ones, you see. The Quality never even think about us – they don't like to, I suppose – and unless we're standin' in front of them with our hands out asking them for money, they pay us no attention at all; they look right through us. So we don't *ask* for money. We slide along like spooks, unseen, unnoticed and unwanted, and we take what we can.' She smiled. 'Then, we disappear, like we were never there.'

'Like ghosts,' said Bram, looking at Molly in wonder. 'The Sackville Street Spooks ...'

The door opened and Shep, Rose and Calico came in, holding a bundle triumphantly.

'Roast chicken!' cried Rose excitedly. 'Mrs Halpert swapped it for three silk handkerchiefs and that lovely Limerick lace collar that Shep bobbed from that cranky looking lady this morning. It was Mrs Halpert's husband's birthday and they had cooked two chickens, but her daughter ain't comin' and her son got a box in the mouth bare-knuckle fightin' at Smithfield Market and can't eat solid food, so they only needed the one. She's givin' the hankies to her husband as a present and she's keepin' the collar for herself, so she looks pretty on Sundays. She even gave us some boiled spuds!' All this was said quickly and in one breath, and when Rose was finished, she laid the bundle on the table, bent over with her hands on her knees and panted. Her Majesty sniffed the warm bundle and started to pant too.

The children happily lifted box lids and looked behind hanging scarves and soon the table was covered in a mish-mash assortment of cracked crockery and bent and tarnished knives and forks. Molly opened the bundle to reveal the smallest chicken Bram had ever laid eyes on – so skinny that he wondered if the poor chicken had died of starvation itself. Then, watched in the candlelight by five sets of gleaming eyes (including Her Majesty's), Molly shared the meagre dinner out absolutely equally onto the plates. She pulled up a crate to sit on and they all, Bram included, dived in and ate the tiny but delicious hot chicken and the small helping of potatoes. Her Majesty sat on the wooden floor and noisily crunched on the chicken bones, growling contentedly as her long tongue licked her doggy lips with pleasure.

Once they were finished, Bram patted his not-quite-full tummy, took the book he had chosen off the top of the book crate and held it up so they could all see. It was a heavy tome, bound in green leather with fancy gold foil lettering. '*Fairy Tales by the Brothers Grimm*,' he proclaimed in as serious and actorly a voice he could muster. 'I promised I'd read you a story, and these are some of my favourites – Nanny used to read these to me in the nursery when–'

'All right, *Quality*,' laughed Molly. 'We all know you're rich, just read the story.'

Bram smiled at his new friend, but did as he was told. Sitting in the near darkness in the crumbling shack on the side of the canal at Mud Island, he read the story of 'Rapunzel' and her long hair, he read 'The Elves and the Shoemaker', and he finished with his favourite, 'The Singing Bone', the spooky yarn about a terrible murder and a magical, singing, tell-tale flute. When Bram looked up from the heavy book, he saw that all the children were fast asleep; while he was reading, they had quietly migrated from the table to their respective straw-filled sacks and were now all snoring gently. Even Her Majesty was fast asleep, cuddled in close with Molly herself. As he lay down in his own sack and reached over for his diary, Bram noticed how Molly's red hair glittered like threads of pure gold in the flickering candlelight.

The Diary of Master Abraham Stoker
23rd of August 1858
Mud Island, Dublin

Well, Dear Diary,

Here we are in Dublin, and the adventure I have been seeking most fervently has sought me out in return.

Already I have taken up with a gang of thieves, risked death and disease in a hellish fishmonger's pit, and been rattled about the noggin by a young rogue's saucepan!

Now I lay that same throbbing head to rest, not on a comfortable goose-down pillow in the dorm at Mrs Harker's, but on a rough sack filled with straw on the floor of a shack that could be best described as 'tumbledown'.

And I couldn't be happier!

Till tomorrow, Dear Diary,

Bram

P.S. I wonder if Mama and Papa are wondering where I am?

CHAPTER 5

ALL THE FUN OF THE (SMITHFIELD) FAIR!

IN WHICH BRAM AND HIS NEW FRIENDS HAVE A FUN DAY AT A FUNFAIR, AND ARE SPIED UPON BY VILLAINS.

SSCHLOORRPPPP. SSCHLOORRPPPP. SSCHLERRPPPP. SSCHLOORRPPPP.

Bram sleepily raised his hand to his face and wiped it. *ICK!* It was wet and slippery! He heard a snuffling noise that was accompanied by a high-pitched mewling growl and opened his eyes to find himself looking into a friendly, furry face. *Her Majesty!* The dog smiled a wide doggy smile and lolled out her tongue. With the morning light behind her, Bram had to admit that the delighted doggo did look quite regal.

'C'mon, Lazybones, time to get up!' Molly appeared, good-naturedly shouldering the dog aside. 'It's nearly nine o'clock. The fair has started already!'

Nine o'clock? thought Bram, *I must have been tired out to sleep for so long – if I were at Mrs Harker's we should be on to our second lesson by now!* He tried to think of what he would have been studying at that moment. *Latin!* He would have been halfway through a double class. Bram sat up and smiled at his new friend and her dog. 'So, Molly, what are we doing today?' His eyes widened. 'Are we going pick-pocketing?'

'There'll be no bobbing today,' said Molly, standing up and brushing curly red hair out of her eyes. 'It's Tuesday and Tuesday is our day of rest.' She reached down a hand and helped Bram to his feet. 'To be honest, I still feel a bit guilty that Billy clonked your coconut so hard, and besides,' she said, 'Smithfield Fair is on today.'

'Smithfield Fair!' said Bram in wonder. 'I've heard of that – there are horses and gambling and swing-boats and bare-knuckle fights – it sounds wonderful! I have always wanted to go to Smithfield Fair, but Papa would never bring me; he said it was full of thieves,' Bram blinked and coughed nervously, 'No offence ...'

'None taken,' said Molly brightly. 'I *am* a thief – the best one in Dublin, as a matter of fact!'

'Molly's the sneakiest sneak thief in the whole of Ireland,' said a tall, scruffy boy as he entered the shack, the morning sunlight gleaming on the saucepan he wore on his head. 'She could steal the petticoats right off of Queen Vic, without her even noticing – her bloomers too!'

Bram's mouth opened in surprise, and he laughed so hard that tears sprung into his eyes. He didn't know whether he was laughing at this young chap's cheekiness against Her Majesty (the actual queen, not the dog) or whether it was the sight of the ridiculous cooking pot headwear that made him giggle uncontrollably.

'Sorry about your bonce,' said Billy the Pan, looking slightly shamefaced. 'I didn't mean to hit you that hard.'

Bram's hand flew to the back of his head, which was still a little tender, but he diverted the hand before it reached its target and stuck it out towards Billy instead. Billy gratefully took Bram's hand and shook it. 'No hard feelin's?'

'Not one!' said Bram, grinning. He beamed at Molly and Billy, his new pals. 'Now, are we going to stand here and chin-wag all day, or are we going to Smithfield?'

❅ ❅ ❅

Smithfield Market was a wide, cobblestoned square surrounded by huge livestock barns filled with farm animals, crumbling and derelict townhouses full of penniless families and grubby children, and tall factory buildings where leather was stretched, glass bottles were blown and whiskey was distilled.

But Bram couldn't see much of the buildings; he couldn't even see the cobblestones. Every inch of the square seemed to be crammed with horses, ponies, donkeys, sheep, cows, chickens and people. Bram thought he had never seen so many people.

'C'mon, Quality,' shouted Molly, over the deafening noise of moos, baas, whinnies, chatter, and what sounded like distant carnival music, 'we've got people to see.'

'But, Molly,' Bram shouted back, 'all I can *see* is people!' She grabbed him by the hand and, with Rose's help, pushed and elbowed her way through the throng, as Bram uttered a string of 'excuse mes', 'pardon mes', and 'frightfully sorries'.

After a while, Molly, Bram and the Spooks reached a clearing in the centre of the square, and Bram could finally see the straw-covered cobblestones underfoot. Makeshift wooden fences corralled in various animals for sale, and farmers and animal traders spat on their palms and shook hands as deals were made. Rose held hard onto Her Majesty's collar as the happy dog tried to jump the side of the pen to play with the sheep. 'She's part sheepdog on her mother's side,' explained Rose. 'C'mon, Her Majesty, leave those lambs alone!'

A few of the people checking out the sheep and pigs looked around as Molly and the gang appeared. They smiled broadly with gap-toothed grins and rapped on Billy the Pan's saucepan hat with their knuckles, each slipping a half-penny coin into Billy's outstretched hands.

'For good fortune,' explained Molly, beaming at Bram's confused face. 'They knock on the pot and they give him a ha'penny for good luck! Good luck for Billy anyway.'

Billy held up his palmful of ha'penny pieces as Shep and Calico Tom looked on in awe. 'This pot is going to make me rich!'

'This way, Bram,' said Molly, skirting the side of the animal pen and pushing her way through the crowd at the other side. 'All the real fun is at the river end of the square.'

As they pushed their way through the bustling elbows, a great cheer went up ahead of them, followed by a great communal 'Ooooooooooooooaaah-hhhh!' Then there was a loud WHAKK-ing noise and suddenly the crowd before the children parted and a bare-chested man stumbled backwards towards them as if he was trying to ballet dance on two wooden peg legs. He stood still-ish for a wavery moment, and then toppled onto his back, completely unconscious, landing with an almighty THUDDD like a pine tree that had just been chopped down by a particularly muscular lumberjack. Another, bigger, bare-chested man stalked towards the first, his fists clenched and growled though clenched teeth. *This must be the actual lumberjack*, thought Bram. A hoarse voice in the crowd shouted, 'THE WINNAAAAHHH!' and another ear-splitting cheer went up from the onlookers, followed by the noisy rustling and clinking of money changing hands. 'Bare-knuckle boxing – very popular, very dangerous and very few rules,' explained Molly. 'People bet money on who's going to win the fight, but when Cornelius is fighting, there's only going to be one winner. Isn't that right, Cornie?'

The huge bare-chested boxer raised his tufty eyebrows and looked down at Molly. 'Ahh, Mol,' he said in a surprisingly high, squeaky voice, 'I didn't see you down there; how are ya?'

'Grand, Cornelius,' said Molly with a wink. 'That old left hook of yours is looking good.'

They pushed on through the crowd, passing poorly dressed men throwing dice against wooden planks, men with feathers in their hats and suspiciously wide sleeves on their grimy coats who were playing games of Find-The-Joker with weather-beaten cards on upturned crates, and people selling apples and cheese from baskets. There also passed by hot food stalls selling fried rashers and fresh bread. The smell of these made Bram's mouth water and he was almost wishing he was back in Cooky's kitchen at Mrs Harker's when Molly tugged his shoulder and pointed. 'Now, Quality,' she said, 'we're going to show you how the Sackville Street Spooks have fun.'

Before Bram was a red and yellow fence with a brightly coloured archway and gate. On the left-hand side of the gate arch there were painted clown's faces, furry blue monkeys, fluttering butterflies and flowers; on the right-hand side there were trumpeting elephants, yellow stars, graceful swans and a picture of a man wearing a big, white wide-brimmed hat and riding a golden horse. A massive colourful steam organ just behind the gate played cheerful carnival music, and behind that there lay a wonderland of huge swing boats full of cheering children, spinning merry-go-rounds with painted ponies moving up and down, and, at the far end, a big wheel that turned slowly, its people-filled carriages swinging gently as they went around.

'Ha'penny per person,' said a skinny boy at the fairground gate. He wore a peaked cap and had the start of a wispy beard on his chin. His eyes widened when he recognised Molly. 'No charge for you, Molly,' he said quickly, 'or your pals – I'll never forget what you did for me Auntie Maureen.' The gang happily trundled through, but the young gatekeeper put a bony arm across, stopping Bram.

'He's with me,' said Molly.

'Another one of the Spooks?' asked the boy.

'Let's just say he's under consideration,' said Molly, 'Aintcha, Quality?'

Bram, who had no idea how to answer that question, walked past Molly and the gang and gazed with wonder around the fairground. Papa and Mama had never brought him to a fair before. *Nasty, dangerous places,* they said, *and very unhealthy for a young boy – full of noisy rides that would make one positively ill.* 'Let's try the merry-go-round,' Bram said excitedly to Molly, 'then the swing boats, and then that amazing big wheel contraption. Look how high it goes! I'd say we should see the whole of Dublin from up there!'

Billy and Shep were trailing a little behind the others when a man wearing a ragged grey coat and tattered trousers blocked their path. A moth-eaten red scarf covered the lower half of his face. 'Da!' exclaimed Billy. 'I thought you were beggin' on the Southside today?' Career beggarmen like Billy and his father were required to switch between the north and south of the Liffey and from area to area every few days; one week a beggarman's patch could be Rathmines, the next he could be sent to Phibsboro. That way, it was thought, the Quality wouldn't feel like they were pestered by the same beggars, day-in and day-out. The roster was drawn up by management and had to be strictly adhered to.

Billy's father raised a gloved hand and removed the scarf. He smiled at his son. 'It's time,' he said.

Billy took off his saucepan hat and WHOOPED

loudly. 'At last!' he cried. 'Can I bring Shep?'

Shep gave Billy a quizzical look. 'Bring me where?' he asked.

'Where?' repeated Billy's da quietly, leaning in as if he had a great secret to impart – which indeed he did! 'To meet the King of the Vagabonds, of course!'

* * *

'I say, Caddsworth,'

'What's that you say, Bounderby?'

'I say, Caddsworth, this Smithfield Market is a jolly rum place.'

'A jolly rum place indeed, Bounderby,' said Caddsworth.

Bounderby's small shifty eyes looked left and right as he stroked his pointy black beard. Caddsworth twiddled his waxed moustache and shiftily looked right and left.

'If you please, Caddsworth, old bean,' said Bounderby, 'would you read the description again?'

'Nothing would give me greater pleasure, old boy,' said Caddsworth, taking a piece of paper out of his waistcoat pocket and unfolding it with great reverence.

'A-hem,' he began to read, 'Girl. Red hair. Blue dress.' Caddsworth carefully refolded the paper and put it back in his pocket.

'The Count is a man of few words, eh, Caddsworth?' said Bounderby.

'As you say, Bounderby,' said Caddsworth, 'the Count is the very *soul* of brevity. He never uses two words when one will suffice.'

'Well, he never uses words at all, dear boy. Have you ever heard him speak?' asked Bounderby.

'I have never had that particular pleasure,' admitted Caddsworth, 'though I have heard him growl on several occasions.'

'As have I,' said Bounderby, pulling at his shirt's starched collar, 'which is why perhaps we should make haste in our endeavour to locate this girl.'

'With the red hair,' agreed Caddsworth.

'And the blue dress,' gulped Bounderby.

The two men stood on their tip toes and tried to see over the heads of the crowd, but as neither was any taller than one of Her Majesty's post-boxes (Her

Majesty the Queen, not Her Majesty the dog), all they could see were bonnets, flat caps and a variety of ill-cut hairstyles.

'A-hem,' a-hemmed Caddsworth, 'I do hate to say this, old chap, but I think it may be time to employ the dreaded Covent Garden Manoeuvre.'

'Oh, must I?' groaned Bounderby.

'We must employ all the tricks of our detective trade if we are to find this girl,' said Caddsworth, 'And find her we must, or the Count, concise as he may be, shall have, as they say, our hides.'

'Very well,' said Bounderby and, laying his silver-handled walking cane on the cobblestones, he got down onto his hands and knees. 'Just be quick about it, old boy.'

'I shall be,' said Caddsworth, bounding daintily onto Bounderby's back, 'as swift as the very speediest and, er, swift-iest steam engine.'

'And just as heavy as a steam engine,' grunted Bounderby, 'OOF! I say!' The two diminutive private detectives-for-hire had devised the Covent Garden Manoeuvre primarily to allow them to be able to see shows in London's West End theatres. They were both too tiny to have a view of the stage from the standing areas, and both too penny-pinching to actually pay for seats, so using the Covent Garden Manoeuvre allowed at least one of them to watch and report back to the other what was happening on stage.

'Can you see anything?' asked Bounderby, 'Girl? Red Hair? Blue dress?'

'I'm afraid not, old boy!' Caddsworth gasped. 'I see her!' he squeaked in a shrill whisper. 'Girl! Red hair! Blue dress!' He began to jump up and down excitedly, much to the distress of Bounderby and his back.

'OOF! Well kindly get off my back then, old chap,' squealed Bounderby. 'Where is she?'

'Up there! On that enormous wooden wheel!' said Caddsworth, bouncing off Bounderby and pointing up to a tall golden-coloured and heavily decorated big wheel that was lazily turning around. In one of the gaudily painted carriages, just coming to the top of the wheel, was a young boy in a soiled grey jacket and sitting beside him was a girl wearing a faded blue dress. Her hair was bright red. The boy was pointing across the River Liffey towards the big beer factory

and the girl was laughing, the summer sunshine spar-
kling off her long ginger curls.

'Hmmm,' said Bounderby, brushing dust off the
knees of his black trousers and squinting upwards,
'she doesn't look like the best sneak thief in Dublin
City.'

'Then again,' said Caddsworth, 'looks can be
deceiving ...'

'As can sneak thieves ...' said Bounderby thoughtfully.

'It's her!' they cried together and scuttled off to
report the good news to their master.

CHAPTER 6

TWO CURIOUS QUESTS

IN WHICH BRAM MEETS AN UNFLAPPABLE FORTUNE–TELLER, AND
BILLY THE PAN MEETS REAL ROYALTY.

R ose walked over to greet Molly and Bram as they hopped off the slowly revolving big wheel. 'That was simply ASTOUND-ING!' exclaimed Bram. 'I could see to the far end of the Phoenix Park and all the way to Howth!' His excitement caused Her Majesty to jump up and lick his face.

'You and Calico should have come with us,' said Molly laughing.

'Well, we would have,' said Rose, 'but Her Majesty is scared of heights.' Her Majesty woofed and Calico Tom snickered.

'All right,' Molly said, brushing down the front of her faded blue dress and pinafore, and running her hands through her tangled red curls. 'It's time to pay a visit to Madame Florence.'

She led them across the crowded fairground, through crowds of children and past a long row of small sideshow tents with striped canvas sides. Each tent was emblazoned with a colourful sign that proclaimed the name and the offering of the attraction within. Bram marvelled at some of the monikers: there was a sign for Molly's large friend Cornelius, the World's Strongest Man; Lady Thimble, the Tiny Duchess of Lilliputia; one sign even promised a personal audience with an individual known as Mangy Moe, the Dog-Faced Boy. Her Majesty barked and growled as they walked past that tent. Outside each tent top-hatted carnival barkers, some with metal speaking trumpets with wide mouths, roared and shouted about the various acts inside, and waited to relieve curious punters of their pennies, should they wish to enter.

Molly hurried past these tents until she came to the second last one. The canvas walls of this tent were striped, but unlike the other tents in the row that had either blue-and-white or red-and-white stripes, this tent's stripes were every colour of the rainbow. No loud-mouthed carnival barker stood outside, and no painted sign hung over the door. As the children approached, the door flap opened slowly, as if by itself, revealing the tent's dark interior. A voice from within said, 'Molly Malone … enter … I have been expecting you …' Bram raised his eyebrows in fright, but Molly casually strolled in, followed by Rose, Calico Tom and Her Majesty. Bram cautiously followed them into the gloom.

The inside of the tent was lit by candles in curved brass holders, hung by metal chains from the canvas ceiling. Heavy, dark-red velvet drapes hung lazily from the inside walls. In the centre of the tent was a small circular table, covered by a blood-red tablecloth with an Arabic pattern of woven gold and silver hexagonal shapes. On top of the table was a large globe made of green-tinted glass. To Bram, the ardent athlete and lover of all sports, the strange glass sphere looked about the size of a football. Behind the table stood a formidable tall woman wearing a long shawl-like dress of golden material that glinted in the candlelight. Her fingers were adorned with golden rings set with large stones of various colours, and on her head was a navy-blue turban with a long orange ostrich feather. Her eyes were piercing blue, and her nostrils seemed to flare as she glared at the children in silence.

'How are ya, Flo?' said Molly, flopping down into one of the red-velvet cushioned chairs that circled the table.

'Ah, not three bad, Mol,' said the woman, sitting down herself and taking off the feathered turban, 'not three bad.' She chucked the turban somewhere behind her onto the floor of the tent. Her hair was greying and, thanks to the turban, sticking out in wild manner. 'Sit down, lads,' said the woman, 'Calico, there's a bowl of water there for Her Majesty if she's thirsty.'

'This is Bram,' said Molly, gesturing to Bram, who

was nervously sitting on one of the chairs. 'Bram, this is Madame Florence, the Seer of the What-Is-To-Come, the One Who Knows All, the Seventh Daughter of a Seventh Daughter, the White Witch of Westmoreland Street. With her crystal ball she can behold events that are yet to happen and with the power of her mind she can spy far into the future.' Bram gulped.

'I'm glad you came to visit, Mol,' said Madame Florence. 'My husband's been arrested for bad debts again and they've slung him into Debtors' Prison.'

'Well,' said Molly with a half-smile and a sideways glance to Bram, 'you obviously didn't see that one coming.' Rose, standing behind Molly in the semi-darkness, tittered behind her hand.

'Very funny, I'm sure,' said Madame Florence, 'It's not Bert's fault he's penniless, he broke his big toe last month and he hasn't been able to do his carnival act. He was trying his best though, he got himself a job in St Michan's Church, cleaning out their crypt.'

'The one that's full of spooky mummies?' asked Rose. Bram's head jerked up and his eyes widened – *mummies?*

'St Michan's is an old church a couple of streets across from here,' explained Molly. 'It's got a vault under it that holds the mummified remains of a thief, a nun, a crusader and loads of others, all lying in coffins, looking exactly like they did on the day they died – just a bit more ...' she searched for the right word, '... leathery.'

'And very dusty,' agreed Madame Flo. 'Bert's job is to keep the crypt free of cobwebs and to dust the mummies, just in case the Quality come in for a gape. The church rector charges the rich eejits an entrance fee to get in to see them.' She sighed, 'The only problem is that there's no money in mummy-dusting. Poor old Bert will be forever paying off his bills there; he'll be in Debtors' Prison from now until the year dot. Not that he minds being in gaol at all really; it's just that it's our wedding anniversary next Wednesday – our twenty-fifth – and I'd really like him to be home for that.' Madame Flo reached over and clasped Molly's hands. 'Mol,' she said, 'can you get him out?'

Molly stood up, stroked her chin and gently scratched the red hair over her ear. Behind her Rose stood, stroked her chin and scratched the red hair over her ear too. 'Wellllll ...' Molly began, 'we can't pull the same stunt we did last time Bert was put away; the guards will be wise to that caper ...' She turned slowly and looked at Bram first, then at Rose. 'Hmmmm ...' she hmmmmed thoughtfully, 'but ... I think I may have a brand-new plan. Don't worry, Flo – there's gonna be a jailbreak and Bert will ride again!'

The Sackville Street Spooks all stood up, said their goodbyes to Madame Flo and marched out of the tent. Bram lingered for a moment, watching his friends leave, then turned timidly to the tall fortune teller.

'Excuse me,' he said in a small voice. 'But, I really want to be a writer when I'm older.'

Madame Flo raised an eyebrow. 'A writer? How wonderful,' she said in a deep, mellifluous voice.

'Y-y-yes,' stuttered Bram, 'and Mrs Harker says that part of being a writer is always to be curious.' He gulped again, 'You said that you were expecting us – can I ask you, how did you know we were coming? And ... and how did the tent flap open all by itself?' He was so nervous he was almost panting like Her Majesty.

'Well,' said Madame Flo, standing to her full height and flaring her nostrils, 'I never reveal the secrets of my phantasmagorical gift.' Bram gulped a third time and took a small step backwards. 'But,' she continued in a whisper, 'if you really want to know: I used a string to magically open the flap.' She pointed to a string that stretched taut across the ceiling of the tent, half hidden in the darkness. 'And I knew Molly was coming because I heard Her Majesty barking at poor Mangy Moe, the Dog-Faced Boy. Very distinctive bark – Her Majesty, I mean, not Mangy Moe.' She smiled broadly. 'Good luck with becoming an author, young man. And thanks for helping to get Bert out of prison!'

Bram thanked her in return and, almost tripping over his feet, left the tent and trotted after the others.

* * *

Meanwhile, in a wide basement of a nearby derelict house, a rough hand removed two black hoods from the heads of Billy the Pan and Shep. The basement was cold and smelled of mould and damp, and was almost as dark as Madame Florence's tent. Shep squinted his eyes, trying to see though the darkness. He got the impression that he and Billy were surrounded by people, but none could be seen in the gloom of the windowless room, and the people, if they were there at all, made no sound. At least, they made no sound to start with. Somewhere in the darkness to the boys' left a gravelly voice whispered one half word, 'Vaga-' This word was answered by many whispering voices, '-Bond'. The first voice repeated his half word, louder now, 'Vaga-' and the crowd replied, louder again, '-Bond.' The words 'Vaga-' and its answering call '-Bond,' were repeated over and over, louder and louder – and louder again – until they became an ear-splitting chant that bounced off the crumbling plaster of the dank basement walls, 'Vaga-Bond, VAGA-BOND, VAGA-BOND, VAGA-BOND!' The volume and intensity of the chant increased until both Shep and Billy had to put their fingers in their ears.

Then suddenly the chant stopped and there was complete silence. Emerging from the darkness,

Billy's da put his hand on Billy's shoulder and said in a gentle voice, 'Billy the Pan, son of Georgie the Shovel, you are in the presence of the King of the Vagabonds – KNEEL!' He pushed Billy to his knees and a light flared up, illuminating the cellar and all the tramps, hobos, vagrants and vagabonds within. Blinking, Billy raised his eyes. Standing before him was the biggest man Billy had ever seen. He wore a long, matted black beard and had huge, bushy black eyebrows. He was almost as wide as he was tall, and the drab colours of his grey and shabby clothes were balanced by the shining brightness of a multicoloured cloak that glittered in the low cellar light.

He spread his arms wide, opened his large mouth, and with a loud booming voice that rebounded from the stone cellar walls said, 'Billy the Pan! Seek ye to join the Brotherhood of Beggarmen?'

'Ehh, and Beggarwomen,' said a small voice.

The huge man, the King of the Vagabonds, swivelled his head downwards on his muscular neck. 'Yes, of course, my darlin',' he said in a softer tone. 'Beggarwomen too.' A small girl standing beside him, barely coming up to his knee, nodded righteously.

'That's more like it,' she said.

The King straightened up and regained his regal composure. 'Well, Billy, do you wish to be called Brother?'

Billy nodded eagerly, 'Yes,' he said, 'I sure do!' Billy's father, standing at Billy's elbow, a-hemmed a small cough. 'I mean,' said Billy, 'Yes please, your Regal Majesty.'

'Very well,' said the King in an echoing voice. 'Then you must complete a task.'

'A TASK!' shouted the crowd of vagrants in unison, 'A TASK!'

'Billy the Pan,' proclaimed the King of the Vagabonds, 'to become a fully-fledged member of the Brotherhood of Beggarmen, I hereby demand that you deliver unto me, within the space of one day ... THE FEATHER OF A PHOENIX!'

'Sorry, a ... what?' asked Billy.

'The feather of a phoenix!' repeated the King. 'You know, a phoenix feather – from the gorgeous feathery firebird with all the, you know, feathers. Them feathers glow like flames, they do; they're right lovely.'

'RIGHT LOVELY!' chanted the crowd.

'So, get me one of them, one of them phoenix feathers,' said the King, 'and Bob's yer auntie, you'll be welcomed into the Brotherhood with open arms.' He opened his arms wide and boomed, 'So speaks the King of the Vagabonds, the one-and-only sworn sovereign of the Brotherhood of Beggarmen.'

'And Beggarwomen,' said the small girl again.

'And Beggarwomen,' boomed the King, but slightly less boom-ily than before. 'Now, Billy the Pan, seeker of the feather of the phoenix – begone!'

* * *

The sun was starting to go down in the late after-noon as Molly and Bram were leaving Smithfield Fair. Bram thought that he had never had such a fun day in his whole life. He was amazed by the crowds of people, filling every square inch of the wide square, and was delighted by the sight of all the different animals for sale, from pigs and ponies to goats and geese. His head was still spinning from the merry-go-round, and his stomach was still swoop-ing from the swing boats. Molly, Rose and Calico

Tom seemed to have enjoyed the day too, chattering happily as they walked down Ormond Quay with Her Majesty sniffing almost every paving stone and cobble they trod upon.

Wandering towards the quay wall, Bram slowed down to gaze at the dark waters of the River Liffey, and his thoughts turned to his mama and papa. They would have known he was missing from school by now. He wondered if they were worried about where he was. He sighed and, turning to catch up with his new friends, his attention was caught by a familiar-looking name on a paper notice that was posted on the wall of a disused building.

'What the Dickens?' he gasped, and ran back to properly read the whole notice. 'Charles Dickens!' he exclaimed to a bewildered Molly as she turned to see what it was that had caused Bram to pull up from his canter like a startled pony. She looked at the notice he was pointing to excitedly. 'Dickens!' Bram said breathlessly. 'The great Charles Dickens is performing in Dublin ...' He squinted at the notice to make sure he was reading it correctly '... tonight!' Molly looked at Rose who returned her gaze with a shrug of her shoulders. 'He's a writer, Molly,' said Bram, 'and more than that, he's my favourite writer – in fact, he may be the greatest author that has ever lived – and he, CHARLES DICKENS, is in this very city right now!'

'I know who Charles Dickens is,' said Molly with a sniff. 'I ain't a total eejit; *Oliver Twist*, *David Copperfield*, all that stuff.'

'Ooooohhh,' added Rose, 'he did that *Christmas Carol* story that I like, didn't he, Mol?'

Molly nodded.

'And he's doing it tonight, Rose,' said Bram, turning from the notice. 'A dramatic reading of it, anyway. It says right here, "Mr Charles Dickens will read in the Round Room, Rotunda, Dublin, on Tuesday evening, August 24th, at 8 o'clock, his *Christmas Carol*!" Oh, I should very much like to see it.'

'That's the one with the ghosts, yeah?' asked Molly, but it was more of a statement than a question.

'Yes,' said Bram, 'and the old miser, Ebenezer Scrooge – the ghosts persuade him to change his penny-pinching ways! *A Christmas Carol* is an absolutely astonishing book. I must have read it hundreds of times!' Bram closed his eyes, took a deep breath, and intoned in a dramatic voice that was much deeper than his normal speaking voice, 'Oh! But he was a tight-fisted hand at the grindstone, SCROOGE! A squeezing, wrenching, grasping, scraping, clutching, covetous, old sinner! Hard and sharp as flint, from which no steel had struck out generous fire; secret, and self-contained, and solitary as an oyster.'

Rose and Molly burst out laughing. 'All right, all right,' said Molly, wiping her eyes. 'As it happens, I know a lad who works in the Rotunda. He's an orderly at the hospital, but when he's not shifting patients, he's shifting scenery in the Round Room. He says they put on shows there to raise money for the hospital; that must be what your friend Dickens is up to. I dare say he'd raise a pretty penny too, if even Rose has heard of him.'

'I'll tell you what, Quality,' said Molly thoughtfully, 'that Rotunda lad owes me a favour. If I swing it for you to get in to see this Dickens fella tonight, will you help me break Madame Flo's Bert out of Debtors' Prison tomorrow?'

Bram didn't even have to think, so caught up was

he in this whirlwind of big city excitement that was as different as could be from his normal life. 'YES!' he cried. 'Oh, Mol, if I get to hear the great Charles Dickens speak, I think I should be the happiest chap in the whole of Ireland – as jolly and joyous as old Mr Fezziwig himself! No prison walls would hold me back!'

'Fair enough,' said Molly, 'I'll see what I can do.' She shook her head and smiled. 'Mind you, I have no idea why he's planning to read *A Christmas Carol* in the middle of the summer though ...'

Bram and his friends cheerfully continued their stroll back towards Mud Island, not noticing the other, rather more urgent, notices posted on the wall alongside the Dickens posters ...

NOTICE:

○

TO WHOM IT MAY CONCERN:

CHILD STILL MISSING

○

IT IS WITH GREAT DISMAY
THAT WE MUST ANNOUNCE THAT
A **CHILD** CONTINUES TO BE **MISSING**

ABRAHAM OR **BRAM**, COMING FROM
A GOOD AND VERY WORRIED FAMILY IN CLONTARF,
IS ELEVEN YEARS, QUITE TALL, WITH
A ROUNDED FACE AND A FAIR COMPLEXION

HE MAY BE IN **MORTAL DANGER** FROM THIEVES,
VAGABONDS OR OTHER ASSORTED NE'ER-DO-WELLS

A **SUBSTANTIAL REWARD** IS OFFERED
FOR THE SAFE RETURN OF THIS CHILD

APPLY TO MR A. STOKER, ESQ.,
THE CRESCENT, CLONTARF OR LATELY AT
TAVISTOCK TOWER, DUBLIN CASTLE

○

MAKE HASTE AND **GOD SAVE THE QUEEN!**

CHAPTER 7

OUT FOR THE COUNT

IN WHICH WE MEET BOUNDERBY AND CADDSWORTH'S MYSTERIOUS MASTER AS HE SURVEYS HIS SINISTER SCHEME.

Bounderby and Caddsworth's pace slowed as they made their way reluctantly towards the dingy, backstreet hotel where their master was residing. By the time they reached Holland's Boarding House with the large, hand-scribbled VACANCIES sign plastered to the front window, they were so full of dread they practically had to drag their feet up the stone steps to the weather-cracked door.

High above them, Count Vladimir Grof-Constantin de Lugosi, Knight-Indigent of Transylvania, paced up and down on bare, creaking floorboards as he awaited his two henchmen in the gloomy surroundings of his fourth-floor room. He moved aside a tattered lace curtain with his long fingernails and squinted through the grubby glass. The moon was rising and, as a few flecks of rain spattered the windowpane, a hungry stray dog began to howl a pitiful HOOOOOWWWWWLLLLL. *Ahhh*, thought Count Vladimir, *the children of the night are calling, what music they make.* He creaked back across the sagging wooden floor, swished his long black cape aside, and sat daintily on the one low seat that the room provided, a threadbare pink chaise longue with spindly wooden legs. He sighed a long, hissing sigh.

The Count had only recently become used to this level of disadvantage and dusty depravity. Back in the old days, he had been rich, proud and powerful. He had been born into a wealthy aristocratic family, and when he had inherited the title of Count, as well as all the family gold, the magnificent horses, the massive swathes of farmland and the huge fairy-tale ancestral castle high in the Carpathian Mountains, he had been the happiest and most good-humoured nobleman in all of Europe. He travelled the continent, clad in fabulous red velvet great-coats with golden buttons, spending extravagantly and living expensively in the finest hotels, inviting noblemen and women to gigantic parties he threw in every city he visited. The aristocrats of France, Spain, Italy, Prussia and every other European state declared (through mouthfuls of cake) that Count Vladimir was a fine fellow, a credit to Transylvania and a most excellent host. Even the snootiest of snooty owners of the biggest and most luxurious hotels absolutely *adored* the Count.

Or, at least, they did until his first cheque bounced.

Vladimir had been spending too much money, far too quickly, and it was disappearing fast. To make ends meet, he found he had to sell the magnificent horses and auction off the massive swathes of farmland. He even had to part with his fairy-tale ancestral castle, high in the Carpathian Mountains – it was bought by one of the snooty hotel owners that had previously so adored him, and turned into, you guessed it, a snooty hotel.

As the reserves of money dwindled, so did Vladimir's reserves of good humour. His hair began to thin and recede, and his round, friendly face became bony and snarly and developed a cold and grey pallor. His bright red, velvet great-coats turned shabby, the golden buttons lost (or, more likely, sold for cash). His arms, previously outstretched in generosity, turned inwards like claws, as if to protect what little he still possessed. Though he had been a tall man, he became bent over, hunched and shrivelled by desperation and disappointment. His cake-loving former friends had deserted him.

In an ill-fated attempt to revive his fortunes, the Count started to gamble away the money he had left by playing cards with disreputable types, and he became known for making wild bets on improbable, near-impossible odds. As gamblers were looked down upon in most cities, he took to wearing black clothes and long black capes so he could move around from forlorn card game to hopeless gambling house without being seen or recognised.

Barred from every card game and banned by every bookmaker in Europe, the near-penniless Count took a random boat from the port of Calais in northern France, bound for he-knew-not-where, and, after several days in the ship's cold hold with only rats for company, he washed up in Dublin.

He sighed another long, hissing sigh. What he needed was gold. What he needed was a plan. What he needed was a sneak thief.

In a rundown tavern in Fishamble Street he met an aged sailor with one eye and breath that stank of tobacco. The wretched old seafarer told the Count about a young girl thief, reputed to be the best sneak thief in Dublin. 'She stole my wooden leg, right out from under me,' said the sailor. 'I didn't even notice till I got up an' tried to walk back to me ship.' The old seaman banged his tankard down hard on the tavern counter, splashing the Count with beer. 'And blister me barnacles if she didn't steal a bit o' me heart too, with her cheeky face an' her shinin' red hair an' her dress as blue as the Irish Sea – reminded me of me own granddaughter she did!'

The sailor closed his one eye and started to sing a

song, 'In Dublin's fair city ...' he wheezed, '... where the girls are so pretty ...'

The Count grimaced and put his bony hands with their long fingernails to his slightly pointed ears. If there was one thing he couldn't stand it was bad, off-key singing.

At the bar the barman put down the grimy glass he had been pretending to clean, threw his eyes up to the rafters and roared, 'Quit yer caterwauling, Renfield, and drink up!'

The sailor was in full flight now, though, 'I first set me eyes on sweet Molly Malone ...'

MOLLY MALONE! A girl, red hair, blue dress. The best sneak thief in Dublin! The Count left the tavern and crept silently up Fishamble Street, keeping to the shadows, almost invisible in his tattered black clothes, until he reached the gates of Dublin Castle.

Looking through the gates, he could see the Tavistock Tower across the courtyard, lit up by gaslight. Two guards, both wearing long red coats and carrying rifles, paraded in unison across the square in front of it. The Tower was famed for housing the magnificent Irish Crown Jewels, given by Queen Victoria herself as a gesture of affection to her loyal Irish subjects. With chains of gold and silver and festooned with diamonds, rubies and huge green emeralds, the Crown Jewels were priceless – maybe the single greatest treasure in all the land. The Count rubbed his scrawny jaw thoughtfully. If he could only get his bony fingers on those jewels – he could break them up, sell the rubies, pawn the diamonds, melt the gold and silver and auction off the emeralds. His fortunes would be restored and he'd be rich again! No more living in backstreet hovels, no more skulking about in the shadows, no more hiding from the many people he owed money to – he would once more be powerful and proud: a Count who counted for something, once again!

His eyes wandered over the round stone Tavistock Tower until they came to a very small semi-circular window above the heavy, padlocked wooden front door. A window that was much too small for a man to fit through; he himself would certainly would not fit, and neither would either of those two idiotic, bungling detectives, Bounderby and Caddsworth, diminutive though they may be ... *but*, he thought, *maybe a small girl could slip in through that tiny window; maybe a small, red-haired girl who is also the city's best sneak thief, maybe SHE could slither in ...* He smiled a wicked grin, his sharp teeth white and shining in the moonlight. He *had* to find this Molly Malone ...

'We found her, Master!' The Count was roused from his thoughts by the urgent whispers of his two henchmen, Bounderby and Caddsworth, as they entered his boarding-house room, bowing low and nervously removing their hats and wringing them in trembling fingers.

'Girl, red hair, blue dress,' said Caddsworth.

'Molly Malone herself,' agreed Bounderby.

'Ifff you have ffffound herrrrr,' said the Count in a crackly voice, 'where isss sshheeee?'

Bounderby and Caddsworth, unaccustomed to hearing their master's actual speaking voice, stammered in reply. 'W-well ...' stuttered Bounderby. 'You s-s-see ...' spluttered Caddsworth.

The Count stood up to his full height, like a curled, blackened leaf unfurling in an ice-cold breeze, and glared at the two detectives with wide, red-rimmed eyes.

'W-w-we couldn't take her in Smithfield Market, sir,' said Caddsworth, bowing even lower.

'T-t-too many witnesses, sir, the Square was too crowded,' said Bounderby, bowing so low his head was almost touching the floor, 'but we found out where she works!'

'Yes!' exclaimed Caddsworth. 'Her bobbing patch is at Nelson's Pillar!'

'Bobbbbing?' hissed the Count.

'Pick-pocketing,' explained Caddsworth. 'Cut-pursing,' agreed Bounderby. 'She and her gang go bobbing at the Pillar every morning, except Tuesdays,' said Caddsworth,

'Tomorrow is Wednesday, Master,' said Bounderby, 'We shall kidnap her then!'

'Verrrry wellllll …' hissed the Count. He flicked them a cloth purse with a few coins inside – almost his last few. 'Go!' he said in an imperious voice. 'I mussst have thissss Molly Malone!'

CHAPTER 8

WHAT THE DICKENS??

IN WHICH BRAM MEETS HIS HERO AND MOLLY MAKES A FRIEND.

After a small meal of bread and cheese at the shack, Molly and Bram got ready for their night at the theatre. Molly tied up her ginger curls with a blue ribbon that matched her dress and washed her face in a basin of cold canal water. Under a large handbag whose label read 'COSTUME JEWEL-LERY – WORTHLESS' Bram found a clean black dickie bow and amazed Rose and Calico Tom by being able to tie it perfectly himself – a trick he had learned at Mrs Harker's Academy, where every boy was expected to wear a bow tie for Sundays, religious holidays and Queen Victoria's birthday.

'Are you sure we will be able to get in?' Bram asked Molly nervously. 'Mr Dickens is frightfully popular, and I am certain tonight's show will be completely sold out!'

Molly winked at her friend. 'Don't you worry about that, Quality. Even if every seat is taken I think we will find somewhere to sit.'

With a wave goodbye to Rose and Calico, they set off down Summer Hill towards the Rotunda Hospital. Bram was excited at the thought of seeing his hero, even if it was from the back of a crowded hall, and was equally excited to be walking the gaslit streets, not with his parents, Ms Harker or any other responsible adult, but with a young thief – a thief he was proud to call his friend.

'I love walking, especially at night-time,' he said to Molly. 'Do you know, I wasn't always able to walk?'

Molly snorted, 'Of course you weren't always able to walk,' she laughed. 'You used to be a baby, and babies can't walk, can they?'

'No,' Bram said, 'I mean I couldn't walk *at all* when I was a child.' Molly looked puzzled, and Bram went on, 'I was bedridden until the age of seven. While other children grew and crawled and toddled and walked and ran, I stayed the same, small and still in my cradle.'

'I was carried everywhere by my mother and by my nanny. Papa made sure I was attended to by every doctor in Dublin and each could find nothing wrong with me. Poor Papa had even called in the famous Dr West of Great Ormond Street Hospital, paying for his passage from London and paying for his stay at Wynn's Hotel in Abbey Street – I'm sure that must have cost a packet – but even the great West failed to find the cause of my affliction.'

Bram sighed, 'I longed to run around like all the other children – I used to watch them from my window, playing across the road in the Crescent Park – while I spent all my time reading adventure books and horror books, and loads of books by Charles Dickens!'

'Time well spent,' laughed Molly.

'Then one day, just before my seventh birthday,' continued Bram, 'my nanny carried me from the house across the road into the park. Oh, I so loved to lie on my back in the grass and stare up at the birds that flew in and out of the trees.'

'Nanny was standing at the gate of the park, chatting to old William, the chimney sweep, when she noticed that I wasn't lying in the grass anymore – I was missing! She and the sweep ran to and fro around the small park, checking every bush and flowerbed, but I could not be found. Nanny became frantic. "My Master's boy is stolen!" I remember her wailing, "Oh! I shall be imprisoned for carelessness!"'

'Where were you?' asked Molly, enjoying the story.

'Ah!' Bram replied. 'Well, just then my nanny and her sooty-faced friend heard a rustle and a giggle from the tree branches above their heads. They looked up to see me, the child-who-never-walked, clinging to a sturdy branch with equally sturdy legs, and reaching out to retrieve a bird's nest. Her loud cry of relief made me lose my grip and I fell down, straight into the arms of the chimney sweep. Plop!'

Molly laughed. 'So you *could* walk after all?'

'Well, I didn't *know* I could,' said Bram, 'but just imagine the sight that greeted my mother when she was called to the hall door – her boy, his face and clothes black with soot, holding hands with a red-faced nanny and a chimney sweep. And standing on his own two feet! My illness, which had confounded the medical establishment of both Dublin and London, had been overcome, as if by magic! I remember Papa saying that it was just as well he put up West in Wynn's Hotel and not the Shelbourne.'

'And so it was that I *walked* into Mrs Harker's Academy when I was seven years of age. *And* so it was that, four years later, I walked out.'

'Well, I'm glad you did,' said Molly with real feeling, 'but did they ever find out what was wrong with your legs?'

Bram frowned. 'Never. Sometimes I still wonder what it was that caused it, and sometimes I worry that the power of my legs will be taken from me again.' He smiled. 'That's why I'm so delighted to be able to walk with you on this fine evening, especially as we are going to see and hear the greatest writer in the world speak!'

'Bram, we've got to pick up the pace,' said Molly, 'It's almost eight o'clock!' A large crowd of well-dressed ladies and gentlemen were politely milling around the entrance to the Rotunda Hospital Round Room at the very top of Sackville Street. Molly took Bram by the hand and led him quickly past the throng of people. They hurried along the curved outside wall of the Round Room to the back of the building where the dim glow of the gas street lights didn't reach.

'But Molly,' said Bram, a little breathless, 'the entrance is at the front of the building!'

Molly raised her eyebrows. 'Ah, Bram,' she said, 'the front entrance is for Quality, not for the likes of us.' She raised her head, put two fingers in her mouth and whistled two ear-splitting high notes and then one equally deafening low note. Bram put his two fingers into his ears.

Above them, an oval window swung open, and the silhouette of a head popped out. 'Howrya, Mol,' whispered the head. 'I thought I recognised your whistle. I got your message.'

A rope came out of the window and fell at Molly

and Bram's feet. 'C'mon, Bram,' she said. 'This is our ticket to see your pal, Dickens!' She grabbed the rope and, arm over arm, pulled herself up to the window. The silhouette's arms came out and pulled her in, then Molly's curly head appeared back out. 'Your turn, Master Stoker,' she whispered. 'Get a move on!' Bram did as he was told.

'Gerry here owes me a favour,' Molly said quietly, as a young boy of no more than ten years of age led them swiftly and noiselessly through a dark passage-way with a dense velvet curtain to one side. A faint murmur of conversation could be heard from the other side of the curtain.

'You can sit here,' said Gerry, gesturing to a couple of wooden crates at the end of the passageway. It was so dark they could barely see where they were sitting.

'Will we be able to see Mr Dickens?' asked Bram.

'I should think so,' said the boy, 'Thanks again for helping out me da that time, Mol. I hope this makes up for all the trouble you went to. Enjoy the show. It's *A Christmas Carol* tonight, even though it's only August and Christmas is months an' months away.' With that, he disappeared into the darkness. The murmuring at the other side of the curtain died down, the curtain pulled back and Bram and Molly found themselves sitting in darkness at the side of a stage, hidden from the view of the huge crowd of ladies and gentlemen who sat expectantly in row upon row of seats in front of it. Then, as one, the crowd broke into thunderous applause and Bram gasped as from the other side of the stage, no more than twenty feet away from where he and Molly were sitting, on strode Mr Charles Dickens himself!

Dickens was wearing an old-fashioned blue frock coat and carried a long feather writing quill as he positioned himself behind a wooden lectern and motioned for the crowd to be quiet. From the lectern he took a white and blue striped sleeping cap, which he placed upon his head. The crowd cheered again. Dickens stroked his black pointed beard and walked to the front of the stage, lit by green candle-light. Bram held his breath.

Dickens regarded the crowd and took a deep breath. In a loud, dramatic voice he boomed, 'Marley was dead … to begin with.' The crowd cheered yet again, and some gentlemen stood to clap. Dickens raised his hands for silence and said, quieter this time, 'There is no doubt whatever about that – old Marley was as dead as a doornail.' Dickens told the rest of his story, of the miser Scrooge's stinginess, of how he was visited by three ghosts, and how they taught him to be kind. He did this without referring to the book at all, although Bram could see a copy, bound in red leather, sitting on the lectern.

'He's amazing,' whispered Molly. 'He knows that whole book by heart!'

Bram thought Molly was absolutely correct: Dickens *was* amazing. The great author waved his arms dramatically, pacing the stage as he became every character in the book; he was crackly-voiced and hunched as Scrooge, jolly and bouncy as a puppy for Scrooge's kind-hearted nephew, shivering and respectful as Scrooge's clerk, Bob Cratchit, and tall and forbidding as the sinister Ghost of Christmas-Yet-To-Come. As he performed, Dickens' face shone with exertion and Bram could see, from his dark vantage point at the side of the stage, the author's hands trembling.

When the 'reading' was over – *if it could be called a*

reading, thought Bram. *Dickens never so much as needed a peek at the book –* Dickens bowed low and the crowd cheered loudly, with many cries of 'Author! Author!' Dickens removed his now sodden night-cap, took his book from the lectern and wiped his face with a handkerchief from his breast pocket. He bowed again and the curtain closed.

❋ ❋ ❋

Dickens sat heavily on the velvet chair beside the lectern, looking wrung-out, exhausted and quite alone. Or so he thought. To the great man's surprise, a small voice piped up from the side of the stage.

'Excuse me, Mr Dickens, sir,' said Bram, who surprised even himself by speaking. 'I'd just like to say thank you for that wonderful reading.' The great man immediately stood and raised his thick black eyebrows. His back straightened and his face, now less wrinkled and baggy, lit up as if someone had turned on a gas lamp.

Two children were sitting, seemingly unescorted, at the side of the stage. Dickens smiled broadly. 'You are most welcome, my boy.'

Bram stood. 'My name is Bram, sir, Bram Stoker, and this is my friend Molly.' Molly curtsied awkwardly. 'I wish to be a writer myself one day,' continued Bram, less nervous now, 'and I have come to Dublin to experience real city life.'

'Have you, now?' said Dickens. 'I must say that is a *splendid* idea! Nothing beats the rough and tumble of real city life.'

'I liked your book, Mr Dickens,' said Molly. 'I've read 'em all.'

'Ah,' said Dickens, 'but I always think that there are books of which the backs and covers are by far the best parts.'

'That's from *Oliver Twist*!' said Bram excitedly, 'I have read that book seven times.'

'Indeed, Master Stoker?' said Dickens. 'Well, to be a writer one must first be a reader, and you certainly seem to be excelling at that.' He picked up his quill pen, opened the leather-bound copy of *A Christmas Carol* he was holding to the title page and, with a great flourish, signed his name. He passed the book to Bram, who looked like he could almost pass out himself, 'Keep reading, dear children, never stop!' With a ruffle of Bram's hair and a polite bow of the head and a smile to Molly, the great writer spun around on his heel and strode off the stage.

Bram stood staring at his new treasure, his favourite book signed by his favourite author, the marvellous Mr Dickens himself. Suddenly his head jerked up and he stared hard at Molly. 'Hold on,' he said to his friend. 'You can read??'

The Diary of Master Abraham Stoker
24th of August 1858
Mud Island, Dublin

Oh, my *goodness*, Dear Diary,
Tonight, I met CHARLES DICKENS!

CHARLES DICKENS!!

Sorry, Dear Diary, I find I am unable to write any more this evening – in my excitement I seem to have broken my pencil, and I am writing this with a small lump of coal and am fownding ut quite duuffic-caulttt tew wriiiiiii…

Brumm

CHAPTER 9

THERE'S GONNA BE A JAILBREAK!

IN WHICH MOLLY AND THE SPOOKS BREAK INTO PRISON AND BREAK BACK OUT AGAIN.

The next morning Bram was woken up, once again, by Her Majesty licking his face. He sat up, stretched and yawned, and snuggled the furry canine who wagged her royal tail vigorously with pleasure. Bram reached into his jacket pocket and took out the book Dickens had given him. He stared at the signature on the title page and thought about how happy he was here in Dublin City, meeting his heroes, having adventures and making new friends. But as happy as he was, he wished he could show his new possession to his papa – Bram knew his father would have loved it as much as he did.

Bram stuck his head out the door of the wooden hut and into the bright morning sunshine. Molly, Rose and Calico Tom were sitting on the side of the canal, their legs dangling over the stone edge. The lock-keeper, an elderly man wearing a peaked cap, was in the tiny garden at the front of his cottage picking roses from a bush, and he gave Bram a friendly wave as he brought the small bunch of flowers back inside. Bram peered around, shielding his eyes against the morning sun. The houses behind the lock-keeper's cottage were built on land so wet and marshy that Bram wondered how they could stay standing at all. No house was taller than a couple of storeys and most of them had a patched-up hole in one of their wooden walls and at least one broken or cracked windowpane. Little pathways of muddy wooden planks laid over the marsh criss-crossed the spaces between houses, and ladies carrying battered wicker baskets held up their shabby skirts to protect them from the muck as they carefully picked their way along them. *I suppose that's why they call it Mud Island*, thought Bram. His thoughts turned to his own pretty house in Marino Crescent – how *lucky* he was to live there.

'Bram!' said Molly as he sat down beside his new friends. 'Nice of you to join us! We're just coming up with a plan for breaking Madame Florence's husband out of the Debtors' Prison.'

'Mol says it all depends on the elephant of surprise,' said Calico Tom very seriously. Rose roared laughing, 'She said "element" of surprise, Calico, not "elephant". There's no elephants in Mud Island; there's none in Dublin except for the Zoo!'

Calico Tom bopped her on the knee with his little fist. 'Give me a break, Rosie,' he said, his lower lip jutting out. 'I'm only six.'

'The Prison is in Green Street, right beside the Court House,' said Molly, 'so there's always loads of policemen around.' Bram sat down on the side of the canal beside his friends. 'Unfortunately, most of them know me,' she continued.

'For bein' the best thief in Dublin!' said Rose proudly.

'Well, yeah, that's true enough,' said Molly, 'but they also know that I sometimes do deliveries for a few of the fishmongers around Dominick Street – so there's no reason I can't be delivering a few oul' fish to the Debtors' Prison. Even prisoners have got to eat.'

Bram nodded, 'Go on …'

She jerked her thumb towards Calico Tom, 'So, the plan is to put Calico here into the barrow, cover him over with haddock and shellfish and sacks and such-like so he can't be seen.' Calico Tom looked at Bram and stuck his little tongue out. 'Yeuch' he said, 'but I suppose it's gotta be done.'

'Then,' Molly said, 'I wheel the barrow into the prison, bold as brass, and distract the guards with a delivery they weren't expecting. Now, usually Billy or Shep would provide some sort of diversion, but they're off on a mission for the Brotherhood of Beggarmen and won't be back until tonight.' She nudged Bram with her elbow. 'So this is where you come in, Bram; there's always two guards at the desk, and I can only distract one at a time, so you're gonna march in from the other direction, dressed like Quality with that snooty voice of yours, slap your hand down on the counter and demand to see one of the prisoners. Those guards will hop to it. They always stand to attention for a posh voice, even if the owner is only eleven.'

'But who will I ask to see?' asked Bram.

'I dunno,' said Molly, slightly impatiently. 'Your father, your cat's uncle, your second cousin twice removed – I'll leave that detail up to you – anyway, while you're ordering one guard around and I'm annoying the other, Rose is going to make a big fuss.' She looked at Rose. 'And I mean a BIG fuss, Rose, understand? In all the confusion, Calico here will slip out from under the fish, grab the bunch of keys from the other side of the desk, find Madame Flo's husband and get him out the back door.' She slapped her hands together. 'Job done, Bob's yer auntie, nothin' could be easier.'

She looked up towards the sun. 'Almost ten o'clock,' she said. 'We better get moving. Her Majesty can stay here and guard the hut. She hates the smell of rotten fish anyway.'

* * *

Molly had been right – Green Street was crawling with police constables when they arrived. 'Keep still an' stop moaning,' she hissed to Calico Tom, 'or the Peelers will figure out that something's up!'

'I can't help it, Mol,' he said in his deep voice. 'The smell in here is 'sgustin'!'

They had picked up the barrow from the back of Collier's Fishmongers in Dominick Street and old man Collier himself had gladly helped them hide Calico Tom under a tarpaulin, covering him over with half-rotten, leftover haddock and mackerel, as well as a few smelly cockles and mussels that hadn't sold and were destined for the fishmonger's pit.

'No problem at all,' he said to Molly kindly, once she told him about her plan. 'Shure, don't I owe you a favour? Besides that, I've been in the Debtors' Prison meself, an' it's a terrible oul' kip. I only wish I'd had the likes of yourself to break *me* out!'

Molly pointed at a big crab in the fishmonger's

window, still alive and crawling over the other fish, 'Would the favour you owe me cover that crab too?'

Molly and Rose had pushed the stinky barrow down Bolton Street, its wooden wheels clattering over the cobblestones and rattling poor Calico's tiny teeth. The crab sat on top of the pile of fish that sat on top of Calico, and Rose had to catch it a couple of times as it tried to scuttle off its stinky resting place. Molly had asked Bram to approach Green Street from the other end, so it wouldn't look like they were all arriving together, and as they turned the corner from Bolton Street she could see him strolling up through the pack of Peelers crowding around the courthouse steps, wearing his expensive school jacket and his bow tie. Molly had to laugh to herself: some of the policemen were even giving Bram nods and half-salutes as he walked by. *Hah!* thought Molly. *One rule for the rich, and another one for the poor …*

Taking a deep breath, but not too deep, *that smell IS awful*, Molly turned the cart towards the steps of the prison, and Rose banged on the door.

'What is it?' shouted a gruff voice from inside.

'Fish delivery!' called Molly.

An eye appeared at a peephole in the dark blue wooden door and looked down suspiciously at Molly and Rose. 'Two kids with a barrow,' reported the gruff voice.

'Open up,' said another equally gruff voice. 'Let 'em in.'

The door opened inward with a long creak and Molly and Rose heaved the fish barrow up the steps and into a short, wooden-panelled hallway. At the end of the hallway was a desk and behind the desk, a wooden door with an iron-barred window.

'Well, well, well,' said one of the guards, scowling, 'if it isn't Molly Malone. I thought you said you'd never be back.'

Molly scowled back at him. 'I said I'd never be back as a *prisoner*.' She pointed at her cart. 'I'm here on official business, deliverin' fish.'

The second guard poked at the fish with his baton, 'ACK!' he said, holding his nose. 'What a stink!' He wrinkled his nose, and then his forehead. 'We didn't order any fish,' he said, looking quizzically at the first guard, 'did we?'

The first guard scratched his head. 'I don't think so, and if we did, I'm sure we'd order fresher stuff – this is too rotten even for the likes of the rotten prisoners here. The only thing that looks halfway fresh at all is that crab …' he said. 'We'll have to check through the orders book on the desk.'

Just then there was a sharp rap at the door. The first guard peeped out the peep hole and started to open it. 'You'll have to deal with Malone here and her mouldy fish,' he said to the second guard. 'There's a young gentleman at the door and it wouldn't do to keep him waiting.'

While the second guard brought Molly and Rose, with the cart in tow, over to the desk, the first opened the door almost graciously to allow the young gentleman to enter.

'Now, remember,' Molly had said on the way to the fishmongers, 'if they think you're Quality, fellas like these guards will bow and scrape and bend over backwards to help you. If you keep your back straight, hold your head up and act like you own the place, these eejits will hand whatever you want to you on a silver platter.'

Bram, remembering her words, strode in with his nose in the air and said in his most upper-class voice, 'You there! I demand to see my gamekeeper!'

The guard gulped and nodded, 'Yessir, at once sir,' he stammered. 'Beggin' your pardon, young sir, but what would your gamekeeper's name be, sir? If you don't mind me asking, sir?'

'Do you really expect me to keep track of all my staff's names?' roared Bram, who was starting to enjoy his new character. 'My father owns the largest estate in all of County Kildare. Neither he nor I know all the names of all of our hundreds of staff!' Bram huffed and puffed in mock-exasperation, causing the guard to cringe. 'He's a gamekeeper, man! He wears tweed, smells of gunpowder, probably answers to O'Brien or O'Leary or some such. Find him for me, there's a good chap; Papa merely wishes to enquire of him as to when pheasant-hunting season is to begin.'

The guard picked up the Prisoners' Roll Book and started to thumb through it, looking for any O'Learys or O'Briens, or even any O'Tweeds he could find.

Suddenly Rose, who had been standing silently beside the barrow, dropped to the floor.

'My nose!' she screamed. 'My beautiful nose!'

The two guards rushed to where she was, flailing around on the floor, with something large, spiky and orange attached to her face. 'That crab!' cried one, 'It's got her by the nose!' He tried to grab the crustacean, but Rose rolled in the other direction, holding the crab tightly to her face with both hands.

'I told you it was fresh!' shouted the other guard, and rushed to help, leaving Bram alone with the Roll Book. Bram quickly looked through the book until he saw the name Florence. 'Cell thirty-four,' he whispered to Molly as the two guards followed a rolling Rose around the hallway floor, her legs kicking out wildly at their shins as she gyrated to the left and right.

'Cell thirty-four!' hissed Molly to Calico Tom, and the small boy slipped out from under the pile of festering fish. With Molly pushing the cart in front of the desk to cover him and Rose wailing like a banshee and rolling around on the ground with the two guards trying to catch the crab, Calico slid silently under the desk. He quickly found a massive bunch of keys hanging from a hook on the other side and, reading the labels, swiftly determined which one opened the door behind him. He stuck the correct key in the lock, turned it quietly, holding the rest of the bunch with his small hand to make sure the other keys didn't clink or rattle. He opened the door, slithered through and closed it soundlessly behind him.

As soon as Molly heard the soft click of the barred door closing, she coughed sharply. At that signal, Rose rose from the ground, right as rain, and tossed the crab to the guards.

'Ah, here,' said Molly loudly, an apologetic look on her face, 'I'm just after remembering, this fish was meant to go to Mountjoy Gaol, not to the Debtors' Prison.'

The guards stood up, dusting down their uniforms. 'What!?' one of them snarled.

'Oh, yes,' Bram cut in, 'and I've just remembered that pheasant-hunting season starts just after St Swith-in's Day. It seems I don't need to see O'Donovan after all. Good day to you, chaps!' He turned and left the prison, followed by Molly and the (now lighter) cart.

'See yiz, lads,' said Rose, following her friends, 'And you can keep the crab!'

The two guards looked at each other, 'Who's O'Donovan?'

The three friends raced around to the back of the prison to find a heavy wooden door opening. A small head peeked around the door and Calico Tom smiled as he saw Molly, Rose and Bram trotting towards him, wheeling the wooden barrow.

'Did you find him?' asked Molly, panting.

'He sure did, little lady!' said a tall man in a white suit, stepping through the door into the sunshine and raising off his head the biggest and whitest hat that Bram had ever seen. 'I sure am mighty grateful to you and your crew, Miss Malone,' he said, adjusting his fine grey moustache and goatee beard. 'I thought they were fixin' to keep me in that hell hole forever! And all over the sake of fifteen shillings in missed repayments on my horse.'

'Happy to help!' said Molly brightly, tipping over the barrow and letting the rotten fish splatter all over the backyard of the prison. 'But we better get along before those guards smell a rat and realise one of their prisoners is missing.'

'I don't think they could smell any rats over the smell of all the fish, Mol,' said Calico Tom, wiping his nose on his sleeve. Rose smiled and ruffled his hair.

'Now, I know Molly here, and I know Rose and Calico,' said Florence's husband as they sauntered away up North King Street, towards Smithfield, 'but I don't think I've had the pleasure of makin' your acquaintance, young sir.'

'I'm Bram, sir, Bram Stoker,' said Bram, looking in wonder at the man's white suit and hat, and noticing for the first time the short, silver-edged cape he wore across his shoulders. 'I've come to Dublin to learn how to be a writer.'

'The name's Wild Bert Florence, the finest Rodeo Rider this side of the Mississippi!' said the man. 'Can I get a YEEE-HAWWWW?'

'YEEE-HAWWWW!' said Molly, Rose and Calico Tom together and giggled.

'Oh!' said Molly. 'I always thought Madame Florence was called Madame Florence because Florence was her first name?'

'Florence *is* her first name, darlin',' said Wild Bert, 'but then she married me, and she became Florence Florence – Florence bein' my second name an' all. The day we married and she became a double-barrelled Florence was the happiest day of my life, yessir! Can I get a YAAA-HOOOO?'

'YAAA-HOOOO!' shouted the gang, and this time Bram joined in too.

When they reached Madame Florence's small house at the side of Smithfield Square, the fortune-teller opened the door and flung herself into Wild Bert's arms and covered his moustachioed face in kisses. 'Thank you so much, Mol,' she said, in between smooches. 'How can I ever repay you?'

'Well,' said Molly, 'you can start by getting inside and making us a cup of tea. They'll be looking for Bert once they realise he's missing. It'd be best if he laid low and stayed indoors for a few days.'

'Good idea,' said Madame Florence. 'Come in, come in, come in.'

While Florence pottered about making tea and Bert looked in a cracked mirror in the tiny dark sitting room, combing his impressive moustache back into order after all his wife's kisses, Molly showed Bram some of the framed posters that the Florences had hanging on their walls. 'Wild Bert was a big name on the rodeo circuit in America,' said Molly as Bram stared at an image of a younger Bert holding his huge white cowboy hat high in the air and sitting atop a horse that was rearing up on hind legs. 'He was a genius with a lasso rope and was an expert sharp-shooter – they say he could shoot a flea off an alley-cat's back at three hundred paces!'

'He still can!' said Madame Flo proudly, as she brought through a tray of tea in cracked china tea-cups and a plate of small biscuits that the children dived on. 'He's still the sharp-shooting, lasso-twirling, trick-riding rodeo daredevil that I married twenty-five years ago.'

'Twenty-five years ago tomorrow,' said Wild Bert, sitting down and grabbing a biscuit before the Spooks ate them all. 'Thanks for getting me home for my weddin' anniversary,' he said, 'and as a token of my gratitude …' He stood up and bent down behind the sofa '… and because we were talking about fleas, I would be so delighted to present you with this fine gift of a flea circus, by way of sayin' a mighty big thanks.'

He put an ornate dark brown mahogany box down on the table in front of the children. It had gold-leaf decoration on the sides, in a repeating circus pattern. The hinged lid on the top had a brass handle and to both sides of that, gold lettering read, *Dr Hopper's Fabulous Flea Circus. See the Mighty Miniature Marvels Perform Fearless Flea Feats.* 'It's amazing,' said Wild Bert. 'Those little critters can do all sorts of tricks – they can walk tiny tightropes, go on miniature merry-go-rounds – heck, they can even ride little tin rodeo horses!'

Rose reached out to open the box, but Wild Bert gently took her hand. 'I wouldn't open it just yet, little lady,' he said. 'That box may claim that the fleas inside can perform fearless flea feats ... but they ain't been doin' much trainin' lately – I ain't been around to do it – and I get the feelin' that those fleas might be feelin' a little like me when I was locked up; why, I was fixin' to jump around and raise hell, and if you open up that there lid, I'm pretty sure that's what they're fixin' to do too.'

'Bert's right,' said Molly. 'Better to keep it closed for now. Besides, Her Majesty's got a flea troupe of her own already!' Molly looked at the mahogany box. *Janey Mack*, she thought. *What in the name of Daniel O'Connell's Great-Auntie Jemima are we going to do with a Flea Circus?*

CHAPTER 10

MOST ZOOLOGICAL, CAPTAIN

IN WHICH BILLY THE PAN AND SHEP VISIT THE PHOENIX PARK IN
SEARCH OF AN UNREAL AVIAN.

'I can't wait to join the Brotherhood of Beggar-men too, Billy,' said Shep as they trudged up to the big stone monument at the centre of the Phoenix Park. Billy took the saucepan off his head and wiped his brow with a sweaty handkerchief. 'Don't worry,' he said. 'You'll be old enough in a couple of years, and you'll get your turn then.'

Beside him, Shep raised up his curly head to gaze at the tall column in front of them and wiped his runny nose with his sleeve. Standing on the column's wide base they could just about see the statue of a bird with long plumage perched on the stone plinth on top. 'Well,' said Shep, 'there's your phoenix, but he's made out of stone. I don't think you're going to get a feather off of him, unless you've got a chisel.'

Billy scratched his head and put his saucepan hat back on. 'This place is called the Phoenix Park,' he said looking around. 'There must be a phoenix bird in here somewhere.' Shep put his hand up to shield his eyes and scanned the wide green fields and pastures that surrounded them. In the distance some deer roamed slowly from one lush green field to another, grazing as they went. There was a faraway noise and the deer suddenly bolted, running as a group to the safety of some trees.

'What was that noise,' said Billy, listening intently.

'I didn't hear anything,' said Shep.

'SSSHHHHH…' said Billy, 'There it is again! It's coming from the Zoo!'

The two boys, one lanky and one short, ran to the

gates of the Dublin Zoological Gardens.

'Listen!' said Billy, holding out his arm to stop Shep in his tracks. They listened again; there was definitely a SHRIEEEKing SCREEECHing noise coming from inside the Gardens.

'And what manner of a hat is that?' asked a uniformed man sitting beside a metal turnstile at the gate. He wore a tall, peaked cap and spoke with a country accent. Billy thought the accent might have been from Cork, but as he had never travelled further from Dublin City than Donnybrook, he couldn't be sure.

'It's a helmet,' he said, rapping on the saucepan with his knuckle. 'Me da got it off a Frenchman when he was fightin' in the war with Napoleon. They're all the fashion in Dublin now. You should trade in that stupid yoke you have on your head and get yourself one of these beauties.'

Shep snickered; he loved it when Billy was cheeky to adults.

'Go on out of that,' said the man, annoyed now. 'Go on, clear off. It's tuppence in and you two don't look like you have two pennies to rub together.' Shep, his tongue out, blew a loud, wet raspberry noise, and the man jumped up waving his fist. The two lads ran off, laughing.

The fence around the Zoological Gardens was high – much taller than a grown man (about twice the height of Billy, or three Sheps tall) – and it circled the Zoo's entire perimeter. The fence served two purposes: to keep the animals in, and to keep penniless poor people out. The two lads walked the length of it, looking in vain for holes or gaps they could wriggle through. 'I thought someone would have tried to make their own "free entrance" in the fence,' said Billy, 'but there's no way in.'

'Hold on, Billy,' said Shep. 'I think I know how we can get in for free.' He pointed up to a large horse chestnut tree. Its long branches, green and full with summer leaves and festooned with spiky conkers, spread out wide and stretched over the tall fence. 'A-ha!' said Billy, and they both started to climb. They shimmied their way across the length of a branch that overhung a grassy space on the other side of the fence, and then dropped down quietly onto the ground below.

'We're in!' said Billy.

'Yes,' said Shep, looking around, 'but what exactly *are* we in?' There was a deep growl from behind them and they both turned.

'Is that a ...' started Billy.

'A lion?' said Shep, finishing Billy's question, 'Brown, furry, big teeth, lovely head of hair? Yes, yes, I think that's a lion, all right.'

Billy gulped. 'So what do we do now?'

'RUN!' squeaked Shep, and they raced away from the lion, towards a stone wall. It was only after they practically ran up the wall, swung themselves over the top and landed on the gravel path on the other side that they realised the lion wasn't chasing them at all. He was lying on his side, lazily and happily playing with a small lion cub. The cub jumped and darted around his father, reaching up with its tiny legs to play with the lion's huge paws.

Billy straightened his saucepan. 'All right,' he panted, 'this place is only for the Quality, you and me will stand out like two sore thumbs, so keep an eye out for park-keepers.'

'And keep an ear out for phoenixes?' asked Shep.

Billy started to nod in agreement when there was

a SKREECHHing noise from the distance. 'This way!' he cried, running up a small hill. They passed an enclosure filled with thick grass, from which small yellow eyes watched them intently. Seals, lolling on flat rocks that jutted out of a pool of deep blue water, honked at them as they passed.

'Shurrup, will yiz?' said Shep to the chubby black and grey shapes. 'We're listenin' out for the phoenix.'

They rounded a corner, and Billy put out his arm yet again to halt Shep. He grabbed him by the sleeve and pulled him into a nearby hedge. 'Park keeper,' he whispered, 'Quick, in here.' They backed into a doorway beside the bush and eased open the double doors with their behinds. They found themselves in a very hot, very wet room. Hot steam hissed from wrought-iron pipes that ran across the room's ceiling and warm water dripped down onto the huge-leaved plants that covered the floors. Along one wall of the room was a row of glass cases. Shep made his way through the foliage and peered into one of the cases. 'This one's empty,' he called back to Billy. 'I'm glad we didn't pay in!' Suddenly a black, hairy, eight-legged form launched itself at the window, making

Shep cry out and jump back, tripping over a low plant and falling down onto his backside.

Billy roared laughing. 'It's only a spider, Shep,' he giggled.

'That spider's bigger than a cat!' said Shep, backing away and giving the other cases an extra wide berth, 'I only like things that have two legs, or four if it's Her Majesty, and I certainly don't like it in here. Let's get out of here, Billy.'

They pushed open the back door of the Spider House and emerged into a clearing surrounded by tall trees with leafy branches. From high in a clear blue sky, the hot sun shone down, warming both their heads. *It's certainly a fine day to be hunting a phoenix,* thought Billy.

Just then, there was a rustle in the branches above them and Billy's head abruptly and unexpectedly became a little bit cooler. 'My saucepan!' he cried, his hands rising to his head. Looking up, he and Shep could see the saucepan moving swiftly along a leafy branch, in the hairy hands of a chirruping monkey. 'Here!' shouted Billy, 'That's my hat, you furry thief! Give it us back!' The monkey EEP-EEP-EEPed a high-pitched screech that sounded to the boys like a taunting laugh. Other monkeys appeared from the leaves and joined their shaggy companion. From their branch they looked down at Billy and Shep, and passed around the saucepan from one hairy pair of hands to the other, turning it over and examining it. A couple stuck out their small pink tongues to taste it and one even put it on his head.

'Look, Billy,' laughed Shep, 'it's your cousin – he's the spit of you!'

Billy shook his fist at the animals. 'Shurrup, Shep,' he hissed, 'that was a present from me da.' Then his eyes widened. 'Ah, no,' he cried, 'not *that*!' One of the monkeys was holding out the saucepan to another, and his furry friend, with a little EEP of satisfaction, was starting to pee into the pot! Billy SCREECHed a SCREECH much SCREECHier than any monkey ever could, and EEP-EEPing loudly, the monkeys scattered, dropping the soggy saucepan and it smelly, wet contents onto the ground. Shep was laughing so hard he had to hold on to a tree trunk to keep upright. Billy picked up the saucepan. 'I suppose I'd better wash this, before I put it back on,' he said, shaking the last of the monkey pee out of the pan. Shep wiped his eyes, his face wet with tears of laughter.

There was another rustle from the branch overhead, and Billy raised his fist, the one that wasn't holding the now stinky saucepan, to shake at the monkeys again. But it wasn't a monkey on the branch this time; it was a beautiful, long-feathered bird. It had a three-pronged scarlet crest on its head and shining, irides-cent plumage that seemed to glow first with a blue colour, and then a bright green. It made a long, low SCRAAAAWWWWKing noise and, with the sun shining through its raised tail feathers, the bird looked like it was ablaze.

'The phoenix ...' whispered Shep in awe. Billy reached his arms up expectantly towards the bird and, to his utter surprise, a single feather floated down towards his outstretched hand. Plucking it gently out of the air, Billy looked down at the feather, long and blue with a fiery eye shape at the gossamer tip, and then looked back up at the bird in wonder. 'Thanks...'

'Oi!' shouted a voice. 'You two! Have you paid in?'

'Time to go,' said Shep, as two park-keepers began to trot toward them up the path. In an instant the

two lads, life-long Spooks that they were, had disappeared into the bushes with the beautiful feather,
and were away.

'They were the two young fellas who were giving
me cheek at the gate earlier,' said the first park-keeper
to reach the clearing, 'They looked like proper little
thieves, the two of 'em – I think they were trying to
rob poor Percy the Peacock!'

* * *

With the 'phoenix' feather stowed safely in Billy's
jacket, Billy the Pan and Shep made their way
straight to Billy's family home in Gloucester Street,
stopping only to wash out the saucepan in a horse
trough as they passed through Smithfield. Billy, his
ma and da, and his many brothers and sisters, lived
in two rooms in a rundown four-storey building
that was home to six other families. Although some
of the families in the building worked as labour-
ers or tailors, while others earned a meagre living
as flower or vegetable sellers, Billy's family were
the only professional beggars – and they were very

proud of that fact.

So, when Billy the Pan bounded up the rickety stairs and burst through the door holding the long blue phoenix feather, Billy's da's chest swelled with pride and happy tears welled in his eyes. 'The feather ...' he said to Billy's brothers and sisters, his voice quivering slightly, 'Today, Billy joins the Brotherhood!'

After many congratulatory claps on the back and ruffles of the hair, Billy's da led Billy and Shep out of the building and they retraced their steps back towards Smithfield.

'Now,' said Billy's da, taking two black hoods out of his jacket pocket, 'you know that the location of the Court of the Vagabond King is a closely guarded secret, known only to sworn members of the Brotherhood of Beggarmen?' The boys nodded. 'Good,' continued Billy's da. 'Then stick these hoods over your heads and follow me.'

With Billy holding on to his da's jacket, and Shep keeping hold of Billy's sleeve, Billy's da led them to the dank basement of the derelict building they had visited for the first time only the day before. He removed their hoods and once again Billy and Shep found themselves standing silently in the shabby yet regal presence of the King of the Vagabonds. Billy's da gently nudged his son's back.

'Oh, King,' said Billy in a small voice. Billy's da nudged him again. 'Oh, King!' said Billy, much louder and more confident this time. 'I have done what you commanded: I have brought you the feather of a phoenix!' He bowed low, holding out the long feather in his outstretched hands.

'How do I know that this is the true feather of a true phoenix?' asked the King.

'He got it in the Phoenix Park,' said Shep, 'It's gotta be a phoenix feather if it came from the Phoenix Park.' The King thought for a moment, then shrugged. 'Fair enough,' he said, and taking the feather from Billy's hands, he stood, swept back his magnificently multicoloured cloak, and stuck the feather in the band of his hat. 'Anudder feather in me cap!' he said with a deep rumbling laugh. 'Welcome, Billy the Pan, to the Brotherhood of Beggarmen!'

'And Beggarwomen!' shouted his little daughter,

and the crowd of fellow beggarmen (and women) hidden in the darkness of the basement, erupted in cheers, whistles and clapping.

CHAPTER 11

THE LIFFEY SWIM

IN WHICH BRAM SEES THE SIGHTS AND MOLLY MAKES
A BIG SPLASH.

The next morning Bram was woken up, not by
Her Majesty licking him, but by the noisy pitter
patter of heavy rain falling on the shack's tin roof. Cool
light streamed in from the open doorway where Bram
could see the silhouette of Rose kneeling, cuddling a
trembling dog and looking out at the rain.

'Her Majesty doesn't like being wet,' said Molly,

tearing off a lump of bread from the loaf she was holding and handing it to Bram.

'She doesn't like being cold either,' said Rose, cuddling the shivering hound a bit closer, and shivering herself as she did it, 'but we can warm each other up, can't we girl?' The bread was freshly baked, warm and delicious, and Bram gobbled it down hungrily. *It's funny,* he thought, *how things taste different in Dublin City.* He couldn't explain why, but ever since he had run away from Mr Harker's Academy with all its wood-panelled rooms, comfortable sofas and plentiful larders, he felt that food was just *tastier* – bread, mashed turnip, roast chicken, and even boring old potatoes. The only problem that Bram could see was that there was simply never *enough* of it here; the Spooks were happy, there was no doubt about that, but they also seemed to be hungry almost all of the time. *Maybe it seems tasty because I never know what I'm going to eat next*, he thought, *or even WHEN I'm going to eat next.* He decided that when he went back to his old life (*if* he went) he would try to appreciate every bite he ate, and appreciate his family's nice, warm, cosy house.

Molly sat down beside him, eating her small share of bread slowly and savouring every mouthful. 'We were meant to be going bobbing today,' she said to Bram, finishing off her bread and licking her lips, 'but there won't be any Quality out this morning, parading around in the rain. There won't be any pockets to pick. So, I thought that instead of hanging around at the bottom of Nelson's Pillar, we'll climb up to the top. There's a viewing platform up there and the views are the best in Dublin, even in the rain.' She winked at Bram. 'It'll be a special treat for our very own member of the Quality, to say thanks for helping us break Wild Bert out of prison!' She rummaged around in the clutter and crates of the shed, carefully shifting the Flea Circus box out of the way, and emerged with some big, battered raincoats. 'These should keep the worst of the wet off us.' Her Majesty whimpered.

'Don't worry, girl,' said Rose. 'I don't think Molly has a dog-sized raincoat, you'll just have to stay here.' The mollified mutt seemed to sigh a doggy sigh of relief.

The Spooks made for a comical sight as they happily plodded their way towards Sackville Street in their oversized overcoats – Calico Tom's was so long that it trailed behind him on the ground, making ripples and waves in the puddles as he went.

Molly had been right about the Quality; it seemed *they* disliked the rain as much as Her Majesty did, and there was not one top hat, red velvet jacket or pleated silk dress to be seen on the street. The only people out and about on this dreary, rainy morning were tradesmen delivering goods to shops and businesses along the thoroughfare, hansom cab drivers sheltering in their own cabs while their horses whinnied in the downpour, some hardy flower sellers, trying in vain with old newspapers to keep the worst of the deluge from ruining their stems, and the Sackville Street Spooks themselves.

One cab, however, was different to the others; it was parked close to the Pillar, and if the children had happened to glance in as they passed by it with their heads down, they wouldn't have seen a damp cab driver taking refuge from the rain. They would have seen two small detectives inside, one with a beard and no moustache, and one with a moustache and no beard. They also would have spotted a crooked, coiled figure with pale, bony features, wrapped in a long, black cloak. And if they could hear over the downpour, they would have heard a hissing, bad-tempered, cackling laugh.

The Sackville Street Spooks, more than slightly soggy from their long walk ('More like a swim!' said Calico Tom) from Mud Island, reached the four-sided base of the Pillar and walked around to the west side, the one facing Henry Street. On that side there were a few steps down to a large metal door set into the stone wall. The door was sealed with a huge iron padlock. 'It doesn't technically open until midday,' said Molly, 'but luckily I've brought me own set of keys.' In the shelter of the Pillar she shucked off her coat, reached into her dress and brought out a set of thin metal tools from an inner pocket. She looked left and right, then got down on one knee and inserted one of the skinny implements into the padlock's keyhole. Squinting, Molly stuck out her tongue in concentration and moved the tool up and down in the wide keyhole. Shortly there was a quiet KRONKKing noise and the padlock popped open.

Molly shoved open the metal door and beckoned her friends inside. 'Take off your wet coats and leave them there,' she said, pointing to the seat inside the door that from twelve noon every day was manned by a cranky, grey-haired, child-hating caretaker, 'Old Joe won't mind a puddle on his chair when he rolls in to work!'

Bram looked up the dark stone staircase that spiralled up the inside of the Pillar. 'One hundred and sixty-eight steps to the top!' smiled Molly. 'You fellas go on up. I'll make the door look like it's still locked; that way we'll have the whole view to ourselves.'

Rose, followed by Bram and Calico Tom started to climb, going higher and higher, and round and round the inside of the Pillar until Bram began to feel dizzy.

'Do you know,' he panted to Rose, 'that this Pillar is actually called a Doric column?' Rose looked around at him. 'A dolly what?'

Finally, they reached the top of the steps, and Rose pushed open the door – no padlock this time, the seagulls circling the top of the pillar weren't as good at picking locks as Molly was – and they stepped out onto the rain-battered viewing platform. A black, chest-high iron railing went round all four sides of the stone platform, and above their heads, providing them with some shelter, the statue of Lord Horatio Nelson, Vice-Admiral of Her Majesty's Fleet (The Queen, not the dog) and hero of the Battle of Trafalgar, stared down at them with his one eye and held a sword in his one remaining hand. Bram ran to the railings and gripped them tight. *What a view*! He had thought the big wheel in Smithfield had been high, but now he felt his head was almost in the clouds! On the west side he could see up Henry Street and all the way to the Phoenix Park, and to the east Bram could see over the masts of the tall ships moored in the port, out into Dublin Bay. *If it wasn't raining so hard*, he thought, *I fancy I should be able to see all the way to Wales*!

'Molly,' he shouted excitedly, 'come and look at this!' When Molly didn't answer, Bram turned from the railings. He walked quickly around all four sides of the platform, but the only people there were himself, Rose and Calico Tom. *Where was Molly*? He stuck his head into the dark doorway at the top of the steep spiral staircase and called her name, but no reply came back, other than a faint echo of his own voice.

Stepping back out onto the high stone platform, he heard a ringing whistle that cut through the noise of the rain like a flaming torch through cobwebs. Two ear-splitting high notes followed one equally deafening low note. *MOLLY'S WHISTLE!* Rose and Calico Tom froze, and then all three of them rushed to the railings.

Far below on the cobblestoned street, wet and shiny with rain, two small, black-clad shapes were carrying another shape towards a black cab. The shape they were carrying was blue, topped with orange curls and was kicking two white legs like a furious mule. Then two white, struggling arms emerged from the blue shape, knocking off one of the kidnapper's hats, and another three even louder ear-piercing whistles echoed around Sackville Street, rebounding off the walls of the General Post Office and bouncing off the large windows of the Imperial Hotel.

'Molly!' cried Rose, 'They're taking Molly!' One of the two tiny abductors bundled their blue, Molly-shaped bundle into the carriage while the other clambered up onto the driver's perch. With a crack of a whip, the tethered horse sprang to life and the cab started to clatter down the cobblestones at high speed.

Bram, Rose and Calico Tom raced down the spiral staircase, reaching the bottom in record time and bursting through the metal door out onto the street.

'There!' shouted Tom, pointing his chubby little arm in the direction of Carlisle Bridge at the south end of Sackville Street. In the distance they could make out a black cab, moving swiftly though the almost solid sheets of rain. They hurried after it, slipping and sliding on the cobbles, shouting Molly's name as they went. A few of the flower and vegetable sellers, hearing the words 'Molly!' and Kidnapped!' took up the chase and ran behind the three friends, eager to help out one of their own.

The cab was still far ahead of the pursuing crowd when, as it was crossing the bridge, a blue shape topped with flaming red hair shot out of the carriage's window, flew over the side of the bridge and plunged down toward the Liffey waters below. There was a distant splash and Bram gasped. The cab stopped for a moment and Bram could see a pale, white face come out of the window and peer into the water. The face then withdrew and, with another crack of the whip and a whinny from the horse, the cab sped off with a tumultuous click-clacking of hooves.

Moments later, Bram, Rose and Tom reached the Carlisle Bridge. They hung over the dripping wet sides of the bridge, trying to see a Molly-shaped figure in the fast-flowing water below, but all they could see was tumbling storm debris being carried along by frothing waves. There was no sign of Molly.

They slowly looked at each other in disbelief, rain coursing down their faces. *Could it be true? Was Molly … gone?*

＊ ＊ ＊

Ten minutes earlier, Molly had been closing over the door at the bottom of the Pillar when two pairs of small hands grabbed her from behind, pinning her arms to her body.

'I'm most *frightfully* sorry,' said Bounderby, as he

covered her mouth to silence her.

'Oh, I *do* apologise,' said Caddsworth, as he grabbed the girl around the waist and lifted her off the ground. The small detective hefted the girl onto his slight shoulders and, with his counterpart peeking out the door of to make sure the coast was clear, bounded up the steps onto Sackville Street and cantered as fast as he could through the heavy rain towards the black cab in which his Master waited.

Molly, surprised as she was to suddenly find herself off her feet and being transported at shoulder height across wet cobblestones, wasted no time in kicking frantically, freeing her arms through brute strength and wildly swinging them about. She began to shout out, but Bounderby, running beside his companion, clamped a hand over her mouth again to stifle her cry. Molly responded by biting down on his fingers, making *him* cry out, and, with a hard punch, sent his black bowler hat flying into a puddle. She brought her own fingers to her mouth and, taking a deep breath, let out her signature whistle: two loud high notes followed one low note. Bounderby tried to silence her once more, but she socked him solidly in the jaw with her fist and had time to whistle one last time before Caddsworth bundled her though the door of the cab. Bounderby, nursing his smarting red fingers and rubbing his bruised jaw, used the wooden wheel as a ladder to climb up to the open-air driver's seat at the front of the cab, flicked a whip at the horse's behind and the cab took off.

Molly found herself sitting (and struggling) on a red leather seat inside the black cab, with Caddsworth still holding her tightly around the waist. The blinds of the two glassless side windows were drawn down and the interior was dark. In the seat facing her was the strangest person Molly had ever seen. He had a pale, skeletal face with white skin that seemed to be pulled tight across a dagger-shaped nose and two cheekbones sharp enough to cut through cheese. He was dressed head-to-toe in black, so it was difficult for Molly to see what sort of clothes he wore, and his long body looked as if it had been twisted and folded to fit into the small space it occupied in the cab. His head joggled against the cab's ceiling as the vehicle bumped over the cobblestones and his long, white fingers bounced in his lap. His voice when he spoke sounded to Molly like the noise of the pages of all her favourite books being ripped out and torn up.

'Yooouuu are the sssssssneeaaakkk thhiieeeeeffff,' he rasped to her, pointing a long and filthy fingernail at her. As it was more a statement than a question, Molly said nothing. 'Thee besssssssssst in Dublinnnn,' the Count continued. 'Yooouuuu will help me toni-iiiigghht to sssteeeeaaaalll the Crown Jewelssss from Dublinnnn Cassssssssssstle.'

Molly shook Caddsworth's arms off her and sat up defiantly in her seat. 'I will not,' she said, jutting her chin out at the devilish figure facing her. 'I may be a thief, but I don't steal for anyone but myself and my friends, and I certainly won't steal for a creep like you!'

Caddsworth gasped. 'I say,' he said, his voice raised to be heard over the rain that battered the cab's roof, 'please don't refer to Count Vladimir as a creep, he may become *(gulp!)* somewhat agitated.'

'Ah, shurrup,' said Molly to Caddsworth. 'I wouldn't steal a rotten apple for this bony-faced buffoon, let alone the Irish Crown Jewels!'

The Count extended his bleached, twig-like finger

threateningly, 'You will doo ittt, girrrrllll, or you will sssssuuufffffferr the connnsssssequencessssssss!'

'Ah, suffer them yourself!' said Molly. She grabbed his extended bony finger with her two petite hands and bit down on it hard. The Count shrieked like a wounded bat and, with surprising strength, lifted Molly off her feet and dashed her against the side door of the cab. Taking her chance, Molly wrenched open the window blind and, before Caddsworth could catch her, she jumped out of the window of the moving cab, onto the parapet and over the side of Carlisle Bridge, disappearing into the churning green water below.

'SSSSSTOPPPP THE CABBBB!' cried Count Vladimir. He stuck his head out the window that Molly has disappeared through and looked over the edge of the bridge. She was gone, *probably drowned*; there was no sign that Molly had been in the cab at all, apart from two bright red puncture marks on the Count's long, pale, skeletal finger. 'Cursssssssses! The Riverrr issss sswollen,' he said to himself as Caddsworth, sitting in the opposite seat, tried to make himself as small and unnoticeable as he could, 'the

girl isssss lossst! Sssssswwepppppt awaay by the riv-errrr. We will have to proccceeeeed without her ...'
Angrily he thumped the ceiling of the cab with his uninjured hand. 'Move on!' he shouted to Bound-erby in the driver's seat and, with a crack of the whip, they did.

CHAPTER 12

THE GHOST OF MUD ISLAND

IN WHICH THE SPOOKS MEET A SPOOK, AND PLANS ARE HATCHED.

Bram, Rose and Calico Tom could hear the sound of Her Majesty howling in the distance as they plodded their way back towards the Sackville Spook's shack at Newcomen Bridge. 'Poor old pup; she knows something's wrong,' whispered Rose, her voice cracking with sadness. 'Ah, Bram, I can't believe she's gone!' Bram put his arm around the sobbing girl's shoulders and Calico Tom slipped his tiny hand into Bram's free hand.

The rain had finally stopped. The August sun had broken free of the clouds, causing steam to rise from the three children's soaked clothes; it glinted prettily off the water of the Royal Canal when they reached the lock-keeper's cottage. Her Majesty trudged over to greet them, licking their hands, whining loudly and throwing herself dramatically onto the damp patchy grass beside the shack.

'I don't know what's wrong with that dog,' said Billy the Pan, appearing in the hut's doorway, 'She's been cryin' and howlin' and mopin' all morning.'

'And she should be barking for joy,' said Shep, coming out behind him. 'Billy's been made part of the Brotherhood – by the King of the Vagabonds himself!' Shep punched his arms triumphantly in the air and beaming broadly, 'Isn't it brilliant? Our own Billy, a fully-fledged Beggarman! Why do yiz all look so sad?' His face dropped. 'Hold on a minute, where's Molly?'

'DEAD!' wailed Rose and threw herself down onto the grass beside Her Majesty. She hugged the dog and her shoulders shuddered as she wept into the crying canine's warm, dry fur.

'She fell into the Liffey,' said Bram quietly, 'We tried to look for her, but the river was too strong; she must have been swept out to sea.' Calico Tom joined Rose at Her Majesty's side.

Billy the Pan took his saucepan off and bowed his head; when he looked up his face was grief-stricken. 'Well,' he said falteringly, 'as the oldest member of the gang, I feel like I should say a few words.' The children gathered themselves into a rough semi-circle and stood looking sadly into the canal water, their hands clasped before them. Billy coughed and snorted back big wet snots. 'Molly ...' he said in a strangled voice. 'Molly was a brilliant thief. Even though I'm older than her, she was like a big sister to me. She was like a big sister to all of us.' Rose started to wail. 'I remember she used to say to me, "Take off that saucepan, Billy, you look like an eejit!"' Everybody was crying now, holding hands and sobbing at the water's edge. Billy took in a long, shuddering breath, 'I wish she was here to call me an eejit now!'

'You ARE an eejit, Billy,' said a voice from behind them. 'Always were, always will be.' They all spun around, and as one the Spooks gave a collective gasp. Standing in front of the hut, with her dress torn and mucky, and wet, muddy leaves in her hair was MOLLY! Rose screamed as if she'd seen a ghost. Then she and the others ran to embrace their friend. Her Majesty jumped to her furry feet and bounced around at the side of the canal, barking happily.

'Molly!' cried Bram. 'What happened? We thought you were dead!' Molly was hugged tightly by each of them in turn. 'When I jumped into the water,' she said, 'my dress snagged onto a big branch that was wedged under the bridge. I got stuck there for a while until I worked it loose, then I clung on to it and floated down the river towards the North Wall – a little Liffey swim for meself, you could say; I nearly floated all the way down to the lighthouse before a sailor spotted me and pulled me out!'

'Those fellas who tried to kidnap me – there was two short little lads and their creepy boss; an awful lookin' sap in a black cloak, *Count Vlad* I think they called him – they took me because he wanted me to steal something for him.'

'What did he want you to rob?' asked Billy.

'Heh,' laughed Molly. 'Well, he certainly set his sights high – he didn't want me to steal two pints of milk and a dozen eggs from Gilberts the Green-grocers! Wait till you hear this – this Count fella has a plan to rob the Irish Crown Jewels from Dublin Castle itself!'

Bram's head perked up. 'Did you say the Irish Crown Jewels?'

'I did,' said Molly.

'From Dublin Castle?' asked Bram.

'That's where they're kept,' said Molly.

'But, Molly,' said Bram, with terror in his voice, 'my father, Abraham Stoker, works in Dublin Castle!' He gulped. 'His job there is the Keeper of the Crown Jewels! He is the civil servant at the Castle whose *job* it is to keep the Irish Crown Jewels *safe!*'

'Janey *Mack*,' said Molly, 'that's quite a coincidence.'

'Molly,' continued Bram, 'don't you see? If the Crown Jewels are stolen, my father will be ruined! He will lose his job; we will lose our home and my whole family will be disgraced! We shall have to move from the city, perhaps out of Ireland altogether, and I will never become an author!'

'Hold on,' said Billy. 'Did this Count fella say *when* he was goin' to be robbin' these jewels?'

'Tonight,' said Molly. 'He said the plan was to steal them tonight.'

'Them Jewels must be worth an awful lot of money if he's going to risk breaking into Dublin Castle to get them, Mol,' said Billy, 'What do they look like?'

'I think I know what they look like,' said Shep. He ran into the shack and came back out a couple of seconds later holding a large red fabric handbag with a flower motif picked out in golden thread on the outside – its leather handle had a card label attached that read 'COSTUME JEWELLERY – WORTH-LESS.' Shep reached into the bag and took out a huge necklace with a heavy golden strap, decorated with gemstones that sparkled in the sunlight. Shep handed it to Billy, then he put his hand back into the bag and retrieved two diamond and emerald encrusted badges; one was huge and in the shape of an eight-pointed star with a red ruby cross at the centre, and the other was massive and oval-shaped with a diamond crown at the top. Shep gave these to Molly and Rose.

Bram's eyes goggled.

'Are they the real Jewels?' asked Calico Tom, reaching up his chubby little hand to touch the glittering necklace.

'Nah,' said Shep. 'I nicked these from the window of a jewellery shop on Talbot Street; they had them made for a display when old Queen Vic visited Dublin a few years ago. When I swiped them, I thought we were rich, but they're not real diamonds or rubies or emeralds; they're only coloured glass.'

'Hold on a minute,' said Molly. She picked some sodden leaves and wet twigs from her curly hair as her brain went into overdrive. 'I think I know a way we can foil this robbery, and give that hideous Count his comeuppance at the same time …' She turned the sparking star with its glittering (but fake) gemstones over in her hand thoughtfully. 'What if *we* break into Dublin Castle, *before* the Count does, and replace the real, priceless Crown Jewels with these worthless fakes?'

'Then the Count would steal the fakes and think he's rich, but he really isn't?' asked Billy, clapping his hands.

Molly rapped her knuckles on Billy's saucepan hat, making a clonking sound and making his head ring. 'Now you're using your spud!'

'But what would we do with the real Crown Jewels, could we keep them?' asked Shep.

'For a while,' said Molly, with a quick glance at Bram, 'just for safe-keeping, of course, to keep them out of the Count's reach – sure, he might try to rob them again if he realises the ones he took were phonies. But we'd put the real ones back once the danger is past; there might even be a reward for their safe return!'

Rose and Calico Tom slapped each other's backs, 'Yes!'

'I don't know, Mol,' said Bram, his brow furrowed, 'Wouldn't it be easier just to warn my father that the Jewels might be stolen?'

'Aaaah, where's the fun in that?' asked Molly, 'Besides, I didn't *enjoy* being kidnapped – I have a score to settle with that Count fella and I am going to make sure he gets what's comin' to him.'

'How are we going to do that, Molly?' asked Shep.

She rubbed her chin. 'Billy,' she said, 'Did you get

into the Brotherhood?' Billy nodded. 'Well done! The Brotherhood are sworn to help fellow Beggarmen in need, and we may be in need later on tonight. Can you get a message to them?' Billy nodded again.

'I need to go visit Madame Florence and Wild Bert. It's time to pull in the favour they owe us. Bram, you come with me. You want to be a writer, and I think this might be an opportunity for you to come up with some spooky ideas.'

Bram smiled and saluted; she really *was* like a sergeant major.

'And Bram, you'd better be in charge of the fake Crown Jewels too,' said Molly. 'Stick 'em back in that handbag, it'll keep 'em all together when we're smuggling them into Dublin Castle.'

'How are we going to do that?' asked Rose. 'We can't just stroll through the gates pretending we have an appointment to take tea with the Lord Lieutenant!'

'Don't worry about that, Rosie,' smiled Molly. 'I think I just might know another way we can get into the Castle.'

Molly's face became sombre.

'All right, All right, listen here, Spooks,' she said,

and took a deep breath. 'The Sackville Street Spooks may be poor. They may be cast-outs, runaways, street-urchins, ragamuffins and orphans. They may be thieves. But remember this: the Spooks are family — *WE* are family. And when one of our family is in trouble, we *all* help out. I have a plan to stop this robbery in its tracks — to foil this Count's plans, and to save Bram's da's reputation. It's going to be difficult, it's going to be dangerous, but, *Janey Mack*, if it all works out the way I think it's going to, it's going to be a huge barrel-load of *FUN!* Now, are yiz with me?'

The Spooks shouted, 'YES!' Bram loudest of all.

'Right,' said Molly. 'Let's get going. And Shep? Can you and Billy bring that Flea Circus box that Wild Bert gave us? I think I've finally thought of a use for it!'

The Diary of Master Abraham Stoker
26th of August 1858
Mud Island, Dublin

Dear Diary,

Apologies for writing in the middle of the day and
not at bedtime as I normally do, but, as Molly would
say, *Janey Mack!* What a day it has been and it's still only
four o'clock in the afternoon!

First of all, Molly got kidnapped by some mysterious Count; she said he was thin as a twig with a face
so white it almost glowed in the dark, and he wore a
long black cloak that wrapped around him like the
wings of a sleeping bat. He wanted Molly to help him
steal the Crown Jewels from Dublin Castle – yes,
dear Diary, the very same Crown Jewels that my very
own papa is in charge of protecting! Molly, of course,
told him, 'No.' *HURRAH!* But then as she escaped
from the speeding cab he was speeding her away in,
she fell into the River Liffey, which was swollen and
fast because of the torrential rain, and we thought
she was swept away and drowned. *BOOOOO!*

We were so happy when she arrived back at the shack, safe and well, if a little damp; and I was even happier when Molly vowed to foil the evil Count's plan.

To that end, we are just back from Madame Flo's where Molly, Flo, Wild Bert and myself have been coming up with a plan of our own, using Molly's inestimable knowledge of the city, along with Bert and Flo's carnival trickery ... and a few ideas conjured up by my own good self! Mister Dickens told me that if I want to become a writer, I must first be a reader – so I have thought hard about all the books I have read over the years, remembering scenes and characters and thrilling adventures – and have come up with some touches to the plan that just may make this Count wish he had never thought of trying to steal the Crown Jewels, had never kidnapped my friend Molly, and indeed, had never as much as set foot (or claw, or whatever he has) in Dublin City!

We have a little work to do here, but soon we leave for Old Church Street to make sure the preparations are underway, and then we travel on to the Castle.

Oh, I do so hope this all goes well, that we can enter

unseen into Tavistock Tower, and that my father doesn't catch us before we switch the fake Jewels for the real ones. We plan to swap the Jewels as soon as it gets dark – so, with any luck, Papa should be long gone home by then.

Wish us luck, Dear Diary. We will need it!

Your very own,

Bram

CHAPTER 13

GOING UNDERGROUND

IN WHICH THE SACKVILLE STREET SPOOKS STORM THE CASTLE, AND BRAM AND MOLLY FIND A GLITTERING PRIZE.

'Ah, Mol,' whined Calico Tom, his deep voice echoing off the curved brick ceiling of the tunnel, 'I'm all wet – the water's coming up to the bottom of me nappy!'

'SSSSHHHHH,' hissed Molly, looking back at the smallest Spook. 'If I'm counting my steps correctly, there's only another hundred feet to go and then we'll be directly underneath the manhole.' In the damp darkness, Bram's foot slipped on some underwater moss, and he put out an arm to the wet stone wall to stop himself from falling, nearly dropping the oil lamp he was holding in the process.

They had entered the tunnel through a circular stone opening halfway down the quay wall of the Liffey at Wellington Quay. 'The Poddle River,' said Molly when they had arrived at the quay. 'It flows from the Dublin Mountains, all the way through Harold's Cross and Dolphin's Barn, then goes underground through Blackpitts and the Liberties, and empties out into the Liffey, right here.' She pointed down to where they could just make out an arched opening with a black iron portcullis gate almost at water level in the stone quay wall. Water streamed out of the opening, merging with the Liffey water a couple of feet below. Thankfully the rain has eased off during the afternoon, and Bram was relieved to see that the Liffey water that had almost swept Molly away just that morning had returned to its normal level.

'The Poddle also happens to flow under Dublin

Castle,' said Molly. 'That's how Dublin got its name – from the black pool, the *dubh linn* that the Poddle formed at the back of the Castle! Now, if we follow the course of the river upstream, for seven hundred and sixty-eight steps exactly, we'll be under the Castle, and there should be a ladder that leads up to a manhole right at the side of the Tavistock Tower!'

'That's incredible,' said Bram.

'Ah, thanks,' said Molly. 'I just know a lot about Dublin.'

Bram shook his head. 'No,' he said. 'I mean that's *incredible,* in that I don't find that story to be *credible* in any way, shape or form. I mean, how do you know all about this manhole at the side of the Tavistock Tower?'

Molly arched an eyebrow. 'Because I can *read* – I think I remember establishing that fact when we bumped into your friend Charlie Dickens – and if I can read …' She took a large piece of paper from the waistband of her dress and shook it out. 'Then I can also read maps.'

She pointed at the paper, tracing a line from Wellington Quay to the Castle. 'This is Messrs

Hardiman & Braithwaite's map of Dublin City, 1858, the Poddle is clearly marked, as is the courtyard of the Castle; and what is that little round thing there, Bram?'

Bram looked closely at the map. 'A manhole?' he ventured.

'A manhole,' confirmed Molly. 'So, if we follow the course of the Poddle for,' she squinted at the map with her tongue sticking out of the side of her mouth, 'seven hundred and sixty-eight steps exactly, and climb up out the manhole – Bob's your Auntie, we'll be exactly where we want to be.'

'I don't want to be there at all,' said Rose. 'That Count fella sounds creepy; and why do I have to be the one to carry the sack of flour?'

Molly pointed back at Calico Tom with her thumb. 'Because Bram's got the oil lamp and his knapsack, I'm carrying this handbag full of fake Jewels, and Calico Tom's too small to carry anything but himself. No offence, Calico.'

'None taken, Mol,' said Calico Tom with a sniff. 'Now,' said Molly, 'there's a ladder down to the Poddle on the other side of the wall, hoosh your legs over and we'll climb down.'

One by one, they sat on the wall, and reached down with their legs until their feet touched the top step of the ladder. Then they climbed down the metal rungs until they were level with the tunnel opening and stepped carefully onto the stone lip of the entrance. Water ran over their shoes, soaking through their thin, holey stockings and making their feet freeze. The walls and ceiling of the underground river were dripping with moisture and green with algae and hanging tendrils of watery weeds. Now and again Bram wrinkled his nose in disgust as he spotted a rat swimming frantically away from them in the slow-moving water ahead, startled by the light from his oil lamp and the splashing noise of their approach.

Now, fifteen minutes of slipping and sploshing later, they were at last coming to the spot Molly had circled in pencil on the map. Bram held up the lamp and, sure enough, there was a shaft rising into darkness above them. Inside the brick-lined shaft, going up into the inky blackness, was a rusted ladder. Molly stepped onto the bottom rung, and it splintered off under her foot, red flakes of crumbling metal falling down into the Poddle water.

'I'll go first,' said Bram, reaching up to the higher rungs; they seemed much more stable than the bottom one.

'No, you won't,' said Molly, stuffing the map back into her dress. 'I'm the best sneak thief in Dublin, remember? You'll probably make such a racket getting the manhole cover off that every guard in the Castle will come running to see what the noise is!'

Molly grabbed one the higher rungs and pulled herself up onto the ladder. She began to climb and was followed by Bram, who, with the handle of the oil lamp clamped between his clenched teeth, helped Rose to carry the cloth flour sack. Calico Tom brought up the rear.

Soon, Molly signalled for them to stop. Above her head, three chinks of very dim light could be seen. 'Finger grips for the manhole cover,' she whispered, 'Put out that lamp, Bram, so the light of it doesn't give us away, and come up beside me here on the ladder. I'm going to need your help to get this open.'

Bram joined her at the top of the ladder and

together they both raised an arm and pushed at the bottom of the iron manhole cover. The cover raised surprisingly easily and relatively quietly. Molly stuck her head up and peeped out. Night had fallen by now and the dark Castle courtyard was feebly lit by gas lamps that provided splashes of weak yellowish light from their perches on the top of black wrought-iron poles.

'No one's about,' said Molly. 'Come on, let's go!' After gently tossing the handbag containing the bogus Crown Jewels onto the cobblestones, she quickly slipped out of the manhole and held the cover open as the others climbed up. Silently they scurried across the cobblestones, leaving soggy footsteps as they went, and hid themselves in the shadow of the Tavistock Tower. 'See?' said Molly to Bram, 'the map brought us exactly where we wanted to go!'

Rose, who was peeking around the corner of the tower, looked back at the Spooks with wide eyes and put her finger to her lips. The children stepped back, further into the dark shadows, and stood perfectly still as a police constable, swinging a wooden truncheon, marched up to the door of the Tavistock Tower and pushed it gently with his hand. The door didn't move. *Locked tight.* Satisfied, he nodded curtly to himself and marched off across the courtyard, walking right over the metal manhole cover that the Spooks had just appeared from.

When he was out of sight, Bram heaved a sigh of relief and the children stepped forward out of the shadows. Molly looked up at the small semi-circular window above the tower door; as she hoped, it was half open.

'Bram,' she whispered, 'the rope.' Bram foostered around in his knapsack and took out a length of strong rope with a shiny grappling hook tied to the end. 'Twelve feet of rope,' whispered Bram. 'Wild Bert said that should do the trick.' Molly took the rope and then took a quick look around the court-yard. 'I wish Wild Bert was around to do this,' she said, almost to herself. 'I'm a sneak thief, not the Rodeo Queen of Lasso Tricks …' The grappling hook made a swishing noise as she swung it around a couple of times, and then she launched it, like a rocket, up towards the circular window. To her amazement, the metal hook flew straight through the window, without breaking the small pane of glass.

'Well done, Mol!' said Bram and patted her on the back.

She pulled the rope back until the hook attached itself to the wooden window frame and, with a wink to her friends, climbed up to the small window and slipped inside. The children rushed to the door and listened. There were a few bumps and a couple of soft *OW*s, but then they heard the soft, scraping sound of a bolt being pulled back and a CLIKK! The door swung open and Molly popped her head out.

'All right, Calico,' said Molly. 'You stay here and get Rose ready for her command performance. Stay well hidden, mind – Bram, you grab the counterfeit Crown Jewels. You say the strongroom is at the top?'

Bram nodded. 'I haven't been here since I was a little child. Papa had to carry me up because – well, because of my legs not working … But the strongroom with the safe is right at the very top of the tower.'

'That looks like it's three flights up, so I hope your legs are working now,' said Molly quietly.

'I just hope we can figure out the combination to that safe,' muttered Bram, 'and I really, *really* hope that Papa isn't still here at work.'

Molly looked at him sharply. 'Don't be silly,' she said in a low voice. 'It's well after ten o'clock at night; everybody's gone home long ago, apart from the guards.'

Molly shut the door silently and they started to climb the stairs. The steps were covered in green patterned carpet and the two friends' still slightly soggy shoes made little noise as they reached the first landing. The doors on this landing were made of expensive-looking dark mahogany wood and were all firmly closed. Bram heaved a sigh of relief. Closed doors meant that nobody could see them as they crossed to the next flight of stairs.

The doors on the second landing were all closed apart from one, which stood ajar. Molly, who reached the landing first, turned and put a finger to her lips. Carrying the handbag with the fake Crown Jewels inside, Bram followed her up onto the landing and they crept quietly across the carpet. Molly stood on a loose floorboard and the resulting

CREEEEEEAAAAKKKK made them both freeze in their tracks, their eyes transfixed on the half-open door. They stood perfectly still and silent for several seconds, barely daring to breathe, until Molly gave the tiniest of nods and they started to creep again.

Bram's eyes, however, were still fixed on the door. He couldn't be sure, but he thought that might be his father's office. It was on the second floor, wasn't it? Directly under the strongroom? He could see the distorted refection in the open door's polished bronze doorknob become bigger and bigger as he and Molly crept closer and closer to it on their way to the last flight of stairs. *Stop being so brainless, Bram,* he told himself, *Papa isn't in the office – he'd never be working this late.*

But as they reached the door, Bram chanced a look inside. *Janey Mack!* There was his very own papa, at the other side of the oak-panelled office, sitting at his desk with his head in his hands. Bram couldn't see his father's face, but something in the slump of his shoulders made Bram think that his papa looked older than he remembered him. Scattered all over the top of the wooden desk were white paper notices and posters. Bram, overcome with surprise and a sudden feeling of sadness at seeing his father again so unexpectedly, couldn't quite read what was written on the posters, but he could just about make out two giant words written in capital letters at the top of each: MISSING CHILD. Bram's father stirred, shook his head slightly and reached across the desk for his reading glasses. Molly and Bram quickly slipped by his office door and stood with their backs against the outside wall.

Molly looked at Bram, her eyebrows nearly reaching her curly red hairline. 'Your father?' she mouthed silently.

Bram nodded. He closed his eyes for a moment and took a deep breath, and then he motioned with his head toward the next flight of stairs. *Come on.*

They climbed the last flight slowly, fearing that every foot they placed on the next step would make a creak or a squeak. There was only one door at the top of this staircase. It was a heavy wooden one like the others in the Tower, but this door also had several sturdy bolts, all of which were open. Underneath the door handle was a wide keyhole and sticking out of the keyhole was a large iron key.

OH, MY GOODNESS! thought Bram. It had occurred to him for the first time that if his father hadn't been working late in his office, the strong-room door would most likely have been bolted and padlocked, and the iron key in the keyhole would right now be in the inside pocket of Papa's greatcoat, hanging on the coat rack beside the front door of 15 Marino Crescent! Molly looked at Bram as if she was reading his mind. 'Don't worry,' she whispered, 'I would have gotten in, even if this key wasn't here.' She winked at her friend and reached out to turn the key.

The lock was well oiled, and the key turned easily. They pushed the heavy door open and entered the strongroom, closing it over again behind them.

'This is the safe where the Crown Jewels are kept,' said Bram. Ignoring the shelves of shiny gold-plated cups, trophies and mounted displays of war medals, he crossed the room to a large green-grey metal safe. The door of the huge box had heavy hinges and was covered in ornate gold lettering, under which there was a big ivory-coloured circular dial with numbers around its edge, from zero to ninety-nine. A small golden arrow painted on the door pointed down to the top of the dial.

'A combination lock,' said Molly. 'I was afraid of that. A normal lock with a key and keyhole is no problem. I'd have that open quicker than an alley cat opens its gob for a tasty mouse – but *this* …' She shook her head. 'Bram, we'd need to know the exact combination of numbers to have any chance of gettin' this lock open.'

Bram wracked his brains. His father would have chosen the combination, but what could it be? Could it be the date of Papa's first dog's birthday? Bram wouldn't have known that; how could he have? He'd never even met the mutt. Or could it be some other date – maybe a wedding anniversary? Bram couldn't think! He paced, looking wildly around the room for inspiration, when his eyes landed on a pile of paper posters stacked neatly on a writing desk by the door. He picked one up from the top off the pile and stared at it. His mouth fell open. The poster read:

NOTICE:

—○—

TO WHOM IT MAY CONCERN:

HAVE YOU SEEN BRAM?

—○—

**TO OUR UTMOST DISTRESS AND AGITATION
WE MUST CONTINUE TO ANNOUNCE
THAT A CHILD IS STILL MISSING**

ABRAHAM OR BRAM, COMING FROM
A GOOD AND MUCH ALARMED FAMILY IN CLONTARF,
IS ELEVEN YEARS, QUITE TALL, WITH
A ROUNDED FACE AND A FAIR COMPLEXION

WE FEAR HE MAY HAVE BEEN **KIDNAPPED** BY
SCALLYWAGS, VAGABONDS OR ROGUE-ISH VILLAINS

A **SUBSTANTIAL** AND **HANDSOME REWARD**
IS OFFERED FOR THE SAFE RETURN OF THIS CHILD

APPLY TO MR A. STOKER, ESQ.,
THE CRESCENT, CLONTARF OR LATELY AT
TAVISTOCK TOWER, DUBLIN CASTLE

—○—

MAKE HASTE AND GOD SAVE THE QUEEN!

Bram stopped reading and whirled around to Molly, tears welling in his eyes. 'I know what it is,' he whispered in a cracked voice, 'the combination code – it's eight, eleven, eighteen, forty-seven.'

'Are you sure?' asked Molly, already on her knees and twisting the dial.

'Quite sure,' said Bram, folding up the notice he held in his hand and putting it into the inside pocket of his jacket. 'It's the date of my birthday – the eighth of November, eighteen forty-seven: eight, eleven, eighteen, forty-seven.' The dial made a soft WHIR-RRRing noise as Molly spun it through the numbers, from eight, to eleven, to eighteen, and forty-seven. There was a muffled CLIKK, and the metal door swung open.

Inside the safe was a single item, a plain wooden box. Molly reached in, took it out and opened the lid. The interior of the box was lined in burgundy-coloured velvet, and sitting embedded in the plush material was a huge necklace with a heavy golden strap, and two bejewelled badges: one in the shape of an eight-pointed star, and one oval-shaped with a diamond crown at the top. 'The Crown Jewels,' whispered Molly in awe. 'Imagine if we could keep them forever!'

'That's not the plan, Mol,' said Bram, quickly removing the real Jewels from the fancy box and replacing them with the fakes. 'We're only minding them for a while in case the Count tries to rob them. That way if he does try, he'll get the counterfeit Jewels instead.'

Suddenly there was the sound of shouting and the shrill noise of whistles blowing from down in the Castle courtyard. Molly ran to a window. 'Speaking of the Count,' she said as Bram joined her, 'I think he's arrived.' Below them in the courtyard guards were running this way and that across the cobblestones, waving their arms frantically and blowing silver whistles. One of them was gesturing towards a tower on the opposite side of the courtyard. Black smoke was billowing from the tower's roof and orange flames could be seen dancing in the top-storey windows.

'He's set a fire as a diversionary tactic,' said Bram, 'to draw attention away from the Tavistock Tower.' There was a clatter of quick, descending footsteps on the stairs and they saw Bram's father run out of the doorway below and race across the cobbles toward the burning tower. 'He's gone out to help,' said Bram. 'That's *so* like Papa.'

A white shape appeared from the shadows beside the Tower door and waved its arms up towards the window, then it pointed both arms in the direction of the door. Molly gave the shape a thumbs-up. 'It's Rose,' she said quickly to Bram. 'She's given the signal. The Count is on the way up.'

Bram closed the safe and whirled the dial around to lock it, then grabbed the handbag with the real Jewels inside. They both moved swiftly to the strong-room door and listened. *Footsteps!* 'He's coming up,' whispered Molly. 'Quickly,' said Bram, 'down the stairs and into father's office – it's empty now that Papa has gone to help with the fire – we'll hide there.' They quietly closed and locked the strong-room door, leaving the key in the lock. With a quick look over the bannisters, they swiftly padded down the flight of stairs and across the landing to the open door of Bram's father's office. They slipped inside and silently pulled the door until it was almost shut, and then stood with their ears up against the heavy wood. They hardly dared to breathe.

Three sets of footsteps crossed the landing. Two of the passers-by had the small, quick steps of startled geese, but the other set of footsteps made a scraping noise as they went, as if the landing carpet was being ripped and rendered by the talons of a giant bat.

Peeking nervously through the iron keyhole in the solid wooden door, Bram caught a glimpse of a crooked black shape with long, pale twitching fingers and a white, dark-eyed face. His own eyes widened and he was about to let out a gasp when Molly quickly and silently clamped her hand over his mouth. Holding their breath, they listened while the footsteps passed the door and climbed the stairs to the top landing. The hair stood up on the back of both their necks as they heard a low, rasping voice utter a single word, 'SSSSSSSTTRRONNNGGGGR-RROOOOMMMM.'

CHAPTER 14

THE OLD SWITCHEROO

IN WHICH THE COUNT ATTEMPTS TO STEAL SOMETHING WHICH WAS ALREADY STOLEN, AND MOLLY AND BRAM GO ON THE RUN.

The Count reached out a bony, white hand and turned the key in the lock. With a push, the strongroom door swung open. The Count looked around the room with squinting eyes. Ignoring the gold and silver trophies, gaudy ceremonial chains and racks of ancient medals, his red-rimmed eyes alighted on the big metal safe. He pointed a pale finger and in a hissing voice addressed his hench-men, 'The sssssssaaaaaffffe, opennn ittt …'

Caddsworth and Bounderby sprang into action. Between them, they hefted the heavy canvas bag of tools they had been carrying in the direction of the safe and placed it on the floor with a KLUNKK. A half-empty bottle of paraffin oil and a box of matches fell out of the bag and Caddsworth quickly stuffed them into a side pocket. He looked around nervously at his master, expecting to be reprimanded harshly for this small mistake. The Count, who was normally surly and ill-tempered, had been especially snappy with his two henchmen, ever since that girl sneak thief had escaped from the carriage and drowned in the river earlier that day. Caddsworth and Bound-erby had felt simply dreadful about that incident, but it seemed to make the Count more determined than ever to get his clawed hands on the Crown Jewels.

Bounderby looked at the safe, took off his hat and scratched his head. 'I say,' he said, 'ever seen one of these boys before, Caddsworth?'

'Of course I have, Bounderby,' said Caddsworth. It's the *Rockford & Garner Four-Seven-Hundred Autolock*;

combination lock, three-inch steel-plated door with iron hinges, five-inch pure steel walls, roof and floor, and the interior offers a generous twenty-two pint capacity – an absolutely wonderful safe!'

'I donn't wannnt you to sssselll itt to meeee, you iiiddddiioooottt,' hissed the Count sharply. 'I wannnt you to oopennnn itttt!'

'Of c-c-course, your Majesty – I mean your c-c-Countness,' stuttered Caddsworth. 'At once, your Lordship!' He looked again at the safe. 'Oh Lordy, Lordy.'

'Bounderby,' he said, 'be an awfully good fellow and pass me that little blue bottle that's in the end pocket of the tool bag, would you?'

'The one that reads *Mister McGuyver's Patented Opening Serum*?' asked Bounderby.

'That's the very one,' said Caddsworth, 'but, Bounderby, do handle it carefully.'

'Why, old chap?' asked Bounderby. He pulled the bottle out of the pocket of the canvas bag and tossed it to Caddsworth.

Caddsworth GASPED loudly, quickly whipped off his hat and caught the small blue bottle neatly inside.

'Because,' he said, giving Bounderby a pointed glare, 'it contains hydro-citronified quadruple-strength sulphuric acid.'

'You see, Bounderby,' he said, wiping a bead of sweat from his forehead, 'the *Four-Seven-Hundred Autolock* is a fine safe, but it does have one weakness.' He gingerly removed the cork stopper from the bottle. Suddenly a strong stench of rotten fish filled the strongroom, stinging the noses of all three miscreants. 'You'll notice,' he continued, holding his nose, 'the steel walls of the safe are quite sound – all of Old Horatio Nelson's cannons would barely put a dent in them – but when the redoubtable gentlemen Rockford & Garner designed the hinges, they made them from iron. And iron, unfortunately for Misters R & G, is highly susceptible to acid.'

Caddsworth carefully dripped a few drops from the blue bottle onto each of the safe's hinges. There was a creaking, wrenching sound that continued for a few seconds, and then, with a KKLLUUMMPP! the door of the safe slapped onto the floor.

The Count's eyes widened, and his gnarled face twisted into what some people (fairly gullible ones with poor eyesight, perhaps) may have considered to be a smile. He reached in and removed the box. 'The Jeewwwwweeelllllllsssssssss,' he hissed, popping open the lid with yellow fingernails and gazing at the box's glittering contents. 'Ssssooooo prettttyyyyy,' he said, almost to himself, 'and sssooo vaaaalluable – theeeeese Jeeewwwwelllssss will ressssstore my forrrrtunnnne and make me ricccchhhh againnnn!' he snarled triumphantly, snapping the box shut and thrusting it at Bounderby, 'Puttt theeesse in the bagggg!'

Bounderby tried to catch the box, but the box fell through his outstretched, nervous hands and its contents clattered to the floor. 'You fffffumbling fffoooollll!' cried the Count, 'Caddddsssssworrthhh, retrievve the Jeeewwwwellls. We musssst leeeeave before we are disssscovered.'

Caddsworth picked up the Jewels, but suddenly stopped. The light from the growing flames in the opposite tower lit up the strongroom, and as Caddsworth stared at the Crown Jewels in his hands, it glittered dully off embedded gemstones. Something was most decidedly NOT right. He held the jewels close to his eye; he sniffed at the connecting golden links, he opened his small mouth and bit the metal of the blue badge. He gulped.

'S-s-sir,' he said. 'I mean, your C-c-countness,' he squeaked. 'I'm rightly s-s-sorry to have to say this, but it s-s-seems the jewels are … oh, how can I put this … fakes?'

'FFFFAAAKKKEESSSSSSSSSSS??!!?!' roared the Count.

'Yes, your H-h-highness,' gulped Caddsworth, 'Phonies, forgeries, falsies, fraudulent fakes. In short, sir, they are nothing but cheap counterfeits, made from coloured glass and tin.'

'Lett meee sssseeeeee!' snarled the Count, grabbing the jewels from Caddsworth, as Bounderby, half-hiding behind the safe from his master's wrath, tried to make himself even smaller than his small self actually was. The Count glared and stared at the jewels. He screeched a long, loud bat-like SCREEEEEEEEEECCHHHH of anger that made both Bounderby and Caddsworth put their fingers into their ears.

The Count stood, crouched over, panting and fuming. His white, twisted face was slick with a sheen of sweat. 'Puttt the fake jewelsss into the bag,' he commanded. Caddsworth quickly did as he was told.

'I say, Master,' said Bounderby, who happened to be looking out the window, 'I hate to bother you, but there seems to be two small children running across the courtyard carrying a large handbag.' The diminutive detective flinched as the Count joined him at the window. They both watched as something dropped from the handbag and the children hurried back to retrieve it. The object was shiny and glittered as it lay on the gaslit cobblestones.

'The Jewelsss!' shrieked the Count, 'Thossse children have the real Crown Jewelsss! They mussst have ssstolen them before we diddd!' He flew to the strongroom door. 'Don't jussst ssstand there, you imbeciless!' he commanded his two henchmen. 'Get after themmmm!'

The three villains dashed down the stairs, taking them two and three at a time and knocking paintings off the walls as they went. They reached the hallway and burst through the front door into the Castle courtyard. The Count pointed a gaunt finger toward the unguarded Castle gate, where two small figures could be seen hurrying through. 'Thatttt waayyyyy!' be hissed, but as they began to follow the two children, a strange apparition seemed to materialise before them, blocking their way.

A small, white figure emerged into the light of a gas lamp. Dressed in a faded blue dress, the phantom girl had white curly hair with dusty ginger streaks showing through, a white, ghostly face and wide, staring blue eyes. She pushed a cart that was equally pale, and a wan cloud of white dust seemed to hover in the air around her. As the Count had pointed at the Castle gate, this spectre now slowly raised a cold hand to point at the Count.

'It's … it's the girl!' cried Bounderby.

'Girl. Red hair. Blue dress,' said Caddsworth, 'but she fell into the river! She's dead!'

Bounderby took his hat off and bit into it. 'She's a ghost come to haunt us for our misdeeds!'

The ghostly girl opened her mouth, and to the three villains surprise, started to sing in a high, warbling, wailing voice, 'AALLLIIIIIIIIIIIIVE! AALL-LIIIIIIIIIIIVE! OOOOOOOOOOOOO!'

The Count cringed in fear, bared his yellowed teeth and turned his red-rimmed eyes away from the horrific sight.

Just then a horse-drawn fire-tender full of shouting firemen clattered loudly across the cobblestones in the direction of the burning Tower, cutting a path between the three rogues and the ghostly apparition with her white cart. When it had passed the phantom girl, and her cart, had disappeared. The Count slapped his two shivering henchmen across their heads, knocking Caddsworth's hat to the ground. 'Neverrrr mind the ssspectrrre,' he said. 'Sssspoooksss and dead girlsss can't hurt ussss – we are letting the livinggg onesss get awaaaaay!' The two small detectives nodded, one pulling nervously at his beard and the other giving his moustache a fearful twiddle. Then the two of them began to hurry toward the Castle gate. Their master followed, his cape billowing in the wind, like the wings of a giant bat.

In the dark shadows at the side of the Tavistock Tower, Rose giggled and shook more flour onto her head from the large cloth sack, causing a large cloud of white dust to rise about her. 'That worked a treat,'

THE SACKVILLE STREET CAPER

she said, smiling at Calico Tom. 'Molly said they'd get a fright, and she wasn't wrong. We slowed them down a bit, all right! The cart was a great idea too. Where did you get it?'

Calico Tom patted down Rose's blue dress and flour sprinkled onto the cobblestones like a fresh fall of snow. 'I found it behind the Tower and covered it with flour. It worked a treat; you looked just like Molly!'

'*Ghost* Molly,' agreed Rose. 'Now let's hope the rest of the plan goes as well as this part did.'

Across the courtyard where the fire raged, someone else had noticed the two children leave, and saw the three figures, two small and one tall but hunched, pursuing them. The man caught a passing guard by the arm and whispered an order into his ear. The guard saluted and the man, straightening his bow tie, set off walking smartly after the children.

CHAPTER 15

'I WANT MY MUMMY!'

IN WHICH MOLLY AND BRAM'S WELL-LAID PLANS COME
TOGETHER, AND THE COUNT AND HIS CRONIES FALL APART.

'Wait!' shouted Molly, over the din of water hoses and bellowing firemen. 'We dropped something!' Bram screeched to a halt and went back to get the Badge of the Grand Master of the Order of St Patrick that had jiggled itself out of the handbag as they ran. He picked up the heavy blue object emblazoned with the glittering emerald shamrock off the cobbles and stuffed it back into the bag. 'Come on,' he said to Molly, 'Rose won't hold them up for long.'

The two friends ran through the Castle gate, wide open now to let the fire-tenders through, and sprinted down Castle Street and on to High Street. Panting, they crossed over the River Liffey by the Old Bridge and raced towards the hulking stone edifice of St Michan's Church. Before they reached the church Molly took a sharp left onto Hammond Lane and kept running, Bram doing his best to keep up. 'Back gate,' she gasped, 'on Bow Street.'

The iron gate opened with an echoing creak, and they bounded up the stone steps and into the dark graveyard, its many headstones gleaming dully in the pale moonlight. As Molly and Bram approached the church door it swung open and Shep stuck his head around, the brown skin of his face illuminated by a gas lamp. His eyes sparkled. 'Are they the Jewels?' he asked, looking at the bag Bram was carrying. 'The *real* ones?' Molly nodded, out of breath. 'Yes,' she puffed, 'but I'll show you them later. We're being fol-lowed, the Count and his two eejit henchmen – is everything ready?' Shep nodded. 'All set, just like we planned.' Bram and Molly, despite their exhaustion, smiled at each other; whatever was going to happen next, they knew it was going to be fun.

* * *

The Count and the two small detectives stood in the graveyard outside St Michan's Church, puffing and panting. Caddsworth leaned on a marble monument, trying to catch his breath. 'I say, old bean,' said Bounderby amiably, between long, ragged gasps, 'you do realise that you're leaning on a gravestone?'

Caddsworth jumped back and wiped his hand on his black frock coat, a look of horror on his face. The Count tutted to himself, *Heh, sssscaaaardeycattsssss* …

The church's stained-glass windows glowed dimly, as if lit from a light inside. 'They are innnsssiddde,' announced the Count, 'and ssssoo are the Jewelsss.' With a sweep of his black cloak, he led the two reluctant henchmen to the door of the church and pointed at Bounderby. 'You firrsssssst,' he hissed.

Bounderby gulped and, with an uneasy glance to

Caddsworth, pushed the huge wooden door and the three villains stepped inside. 'Oh dear, Caddsworth,' whispered Bounderby, 'this old church looks d-d-decidedly c-c-creepy.' Caddsworth nodded. 'Not to mention p-p-positively un-p-p-pleasant.'

The interior of the church was dark and cold. Lit candles lined the side walls, providing a flickering yellow light that danced off the rows of wooden pews leading to the large, ornamented altar. The Count looked from left to right and hissed a low HISSSSSSSSSSSS. The church seemed to be completely empty.

A small creak made the two jittery detectives jump and clutch each other and they turned as one to find the source of the noise: a wrought-iron gate in an arched stone doorway behind them was ajar and moving slightly. 'Thissssss waaaayyyyy,' said the Count and dragged his unwilling henchman to the doorway in the church wall. He pointed at the gate.

'Let me g-g-guess,' stuttered Bounderby, 'm-m-me first?'

The Count nodded.

Bounderby opened the gate. At the other side

were steep, stone steps that descended into darkness. Caddsworth looked back at his master, but the Count urged them on with flaring eyes. They moved slowly down the steps, none of them noticing a black painted sign on the wall that read CRYPT in golden letters.

If the stairs down were dark, the cold, echoing chamber at the bottom was even darker – a pitch black that made the two small henchmen shiver, while the stale air within had a frigid chill that made their teeth chatter.

The Count reached blindly into his cloak and found, in an inside pocket, a box of matches. With long, bony fingers he stretched out and found a stone wall, and struck a match against it, igniting the small flame. Holding it high in the freezing air, he could see old, dusty wooden boxes piled on top of each other around the walls, but no sign at all of any children, or the Jewels he was sure they were carrying. *Currrrsssesssssss.*

There was a small puff of air and the match's flame extinguished, leaving the Count and his henchmen again in sudden, total darkness.

Then the whole chamber lit up unexpectedly with an unearthly, glowing green light. A huge, incandescent form reared over the wooden boxes and glowered at the Count with flaming eyes. The figure was tall, its head almost reaching the arched ceiling of the crypt, and it wore flowing, net-like robes that seemed to billow as if caught in the eddies of an icy breeze that neither Caddsworth nor Bounderby could feel. Its arms were outstretched, and held CLANKKing lengths of heavy chain, held together with rusty iron padlocks. As the villains stared with wide eyes, the monstrous figure opened its mouth and, without moving its lips, began to speak.

'I wear the chain I forged in life,' it roared in a deep, booming voice, its mouth completely still, a perfectly round O. 'I made it link by link, and yard by yard; I girded it on of my own free will, and of my own free will I wore it.'

The figure held out the chains to the Count and his terrified cronies. 'YOU!' he wailed, 'You will be visited by three spirits! The first you have met …'

The figure opened his billowing cloak. To the horror of Bounderby and Caddsworth, a white-faced Molly Malone appeared from under the tattered fabric. She glared at the villains, surrounded by a white cloud of dust, and moaned a long MOOOAAAANNN.

'... and two more you have yet to meet!' continued the glowing figure, gesturing to the wooden box-like coffins at his feet. With a slow, spooky KKREEEEAAAAAKKKKK, the lids of two of the boxes began to rise, and, with juddering motions, two skeletal mummies dressed in grey rags began to sit up, the brown, leathery skin of their faces shining in the eerie green light.

Bounderby and Caddsworth screamed in high-pitched, shrieking voices and ran for the stairs, reaching the top in record time and bursting through the crypt gate into the church, with the Count not far behind them.

The giant green figure dropped the chains to the floor with a CLANK and took off his flowing cloak of coloured silk handkerchiefs. 'How did I do, Flo?' the figure asked in a high, squeaky voice. 'You were great, Cornelius, the biggest ghost any of those nitwits ever saw!' said Madame Florence, peeping out from behind a tall pile of coffins. 'And you did a grand job too, Bram,' she said as Bram stepped out of the shadows, grinning and holding a metal megaphone. 'Great acting skills! And if you ever want to become a carnival barker, give me a shout!' Then, with a small, ladylike grunt, she eased back on the rope she was holding and the two mummies that had been sitting up so scarily, lay back down gently into their coffins.

Reaching the top of the steps, the Count emerged into the nave with his black cloak torn and flapping behind him. The candles had been extinguished and the interior of the church was in near-total darkness, with only moonlight coming through the stained-glass windows from outside.

In the dimness the Count could see movement from the wooden seats at the front of the church. There was a scratching, skittering noise and a dark misshapen form seemed to slowly creep toward them, moving in jerky motions down the centre aisle. A spotlight suddenly illuminated the strange mass of black limbs that was drawing closer and Bounderby and Caddsworth screamed again. It was a massive, black, eight-legged spider! The enormous insect's dark, spiky legs seemed to be covered in sharp, shaggy fur, and an untold number of shiny eyes glinted evilly at them in the moonlight. It made a low growling noise and kept moving towards them.

'The dooooorrr …!' mewled the Count in a small voice, and the three villains, as one, backed away from the monstrous shape that bore down so relentlessly upon them, and stepped backwards, one petrified step at a time, towards the church door and escape. As they reached blindly behind them for the door's wood panelling, they almost didn't notice a strange rain of tiny, nearly weightless objects that pitter-pattered down onto their heads and shoulders. One of the small, brown creatures found its way under the collar of Count Vladimir's cloak and onto the back of his neck. There, the minuscule monster bit into the Count's flesh with the tiniest of teeth. The Count stood completely upright and slapped his bony hand onto the back of his neck.

'AAAIIIEEEEE!! BLOODSUCKERS!!!' he squealed. 'I have been bitten by a FLEA!' Caddsworth and Bounderby started to jerk this way and that, slapping and scratching at themselves as the fleas that had been emptied onto their heads began to burrow under their clothing and make them itch uncontrollably. In the choir balcony above, Shep and Calico Tom giggled quietly as, unseen by the villains below, they shook the last of the fleas out of the Flea Circus box.

The Count, pawing at his tummy and back and legs simultaneously with his skeletal fingernails, managed to pull the church door open and the three itchy miscreants stumbled out into the cold night air. They fell to their knees, scratching at the fleas that were running up and down the insides of every article of clothing and hopping happily from one twitching, wretched villain to the other.

'AALLLIIIIIIIVE!' called a voice from the grave-yard, and the spectral form of a white-faced Molly Malone rose slowly from behind a headstone. 'AAL-LLIIIIIIIIVE!' answered another voice, and another white-faced phantom Molly stepped from the door-way of the church.

'OOOOOOOOOOOO!!!!' cried Caddsworth and Bounderby together and, staggering to their feet, they tottered down the stone steps to the church gate, leaving the Count behind, alone with the two spooks.

'I'm f-f-f-frightfully sorry to have to say this, Master,' cried Caddsworth.

'... B-b-but I fear we must t-t-tender our r-r-resignations ...,' shouted Bounderby.

'W-w-with immediate effect!' concluded Caddsworth.

They flew through the church gate and clattered a few steps up the cobblestones of Bow Street until they were stopped in their tracks by a magnificent white horse, on top of which sat a cowboy, wearing a huge white hat and swinging a lasso rope around his head. 'YEEEEE-HAAAAWWWW!' yelled the cowboy, 'Wild Bert Florence rides again!' The two henchman tried to flee, but the horse reared up on his hind legs, neighing loudly. Wild Bert flung the rope he was twirling and lassoed them both around their chests, trapping them tight in one big loop of rope.

The Count, for once following his idiotic henchmen's lead, made it to the bottom of the churchyard steps. He was slinking through the gate when, from out of the shadows of Bow Street, a huge crowd materialised. At the head of this rag-tag, shabby crowd of people was the King of the Vagabonds himself, tall and proud and wearing a hat with a 'phoenix' feather fluttering from the side. Beside him was Billy the Pan, wearing a gleaming hat that was, well, a saucepan. In a loud, clear voice, Billy started to speak. 'Stop in the name of the Brotherhood!' he began.

'And *Sisterhood*,' interjected a small voice.

Billy smiled down at the tiny girl standing beside the King, 'And *Sister*hood of Beggarmen!'

The little girl stamped her foot. 'And don't forget the Beggarwomen!'

The King of the Vagabonds put his hand on his daughter's shoulder. 'Hear, hear,' he said, and they both gave the Count the dirtiest looks they could muster.

Count Vladimir Grof-Constantin de Lugosi, Knight-Indigent of Transylvania, faced by what seemed like a ragged army of Beggarmen (and Beggarwomen!), and with his henchmen tied up by a cowboy on a massive white horse, knew he was beaten. He slumped where he stood, his shoulders drooping.

Bram and Molly walked down the stone steps and into the street. Molly shook flour dust from her hair as Rose came up beside her doing the same thing while trying to hold Her Majesty, eight-legged in her home-made spider costume and barking happily. Shep and Calico Tom joined the other Sackville Street Spooks and, between them, held up the handbag with the real Irish Crown Jewels inside. Molly pointed at the bag, a big smile spreading across her face as she looked directly into the Count's red-rimmed eyes. 'Looking for these?' she asked.

At that moment a troop of guards rounded the corner from Hammond Lane. Their uniforms were blackened with soot, and they carried with them a smell of smoke and burnt wood. The Brotherhood (and Sisterhood) of Beggarmen (and Beggarwomen) stepped back silently into the shadows at the side of the street and vanished, as if they had never been there, leaving only Madame Flo, Wild Bert on his horse, and Bram and the Sackville Street Spooks standing on the cobblestones, with the Count and his defeated henchmen, sitting on the ground between them.

A tall, bearded gentleman pushed his way through the sooty troop. 'Bram?' he gasped in a cracked voice. 'Is it you?'

'PAPA!' cried Bram Stoker and ran into the arms of his father. The older Stoker held his son tight and kissed him on the forehead.

'These men,' said Bram urgently, wrestling himself from his father's grip, 'these men, Papa, they're the ones who set fire to the tower!' Papa Stoker furrowed his eyebrows in puzzlement, looking at the three pathetic figures on the ground.

'It's true, your honour,' said Molly, stepping forward. 'Check that man's bag.' Caddsworth looked down at the bag he was carrying in surprise; in all the excitement he had forgotten completely that he was still holding it. Papa Stoker marched over and grabbed the bag. He turned it upside down to empty it, and a hammer, a chisel and an iron crowbar clattered out onto the cobbles, followed by a bottle of paraffin and a box of matches. The fake Crown Jewels were the last things to fall out of the bag, and they lay on the ground, glittering in the lamp light. Papa Stoker staggered back. 'The Crown Jewels!' he cried. 'You villains set a tower ablaze, just as a distraction, while you tried to steal the Irish Crown Jewels?!'

'He *told* us to do it!' cried Caddsworth, pointing at the Count and nervously twiddling his moustache.

'As a point of fact, he *made* us do it, he was quite insistent!' cried Bounderby, gesturing his head in the Count's direction as he nervously tugged at his beard. The Count hissed at them, baring his yellow teeth and dragging his tattered cloak around him, like a bat preparing to sleep.

'Take them away, men!' ordered Papa Stoker, 'Charge them with arson and the attempted theft of the Irish Crown Jewels.'

Bram's eyes widened as his father picked up the fake Crown Jewels and put them back into the bag. 'I don't know what we would have done if these had been stolen,' he said, almost to himself. 'My reputation would have been in ruins …' Then Papa Stoker turned his full attention to his son. 'And now, Bram, my boy, I think you and your new friends have a little bit of explaining to do.'

Bram looked around for his friends, but Molly Malone and the Sackville Street Spooks were nowhere to be seen – even Madame Flo and Wild Bert on his white horse were gone. They had all disappeared into the night – quietly, swiftly and silently.

Just like ghosts.

The Diary of Master Abraham Stoker

31st of August 1858

15 Marino Crescent, Clontarf

Dear Diary,

Although I can't express how wonderful it is to be sleeping once again in my own bed, with my own bed linen, my own pillow, and my very own signed copy of Charles Dickens' 'A Christmas Carol' resting in pride of place on my bedside table, I also find it hard to tell you how much I miss Molly and the rest of her little gang of thieves: Rose with her red hair just like Mol's, Shep with his runny nose and big brown eyes, Calico Tom with his baby face and his ridiculous nappy. I even miss Billy the Pan, despite the fact that he clonked me quite hard on the noggin.

I have made a solemn promise to Mama to never run away again; she is so glad to have me back safe and sound. As is Papa.

Papa is also glad to have the Crown Jewels back safe and sound. He took them off the Count and locked them up again in his strongroom, in a brand new guaranteed-unbreakable-into safe. The Count and his cronies are in prison now, Papa tells me – he says the Count is teaching the other prisoners how to play poker and is boasting to everyone about how he almost stole the Irish Crown Jewels. He actually seems to be perfectly happy in prison and has become quite the celebrity. I shall never forget the first time I set eyes on the chap, with his pinched white face, his black cloak and his long, bony hands. Do you know, Dear Diary, he *may* make a good character for a book someday. Or, more likely, an *evil* character ...

I simply haven't the heart to tell Papa the jewels he locked away are fakes.

And the real Irish Crown Jewels? The ceremonial chains and badges of precious gold and silver, encrusted with priceless diamonds, rubies and emeralds?

I don't know where they are.

But if I had to guess ... I'd say that my good and dear friend Molly Malone might have them in her possession. Maybe minus one or two diamonds, if the letter I received from her is anything to go by.

Dear Bram,
Greetings from Plymouth Harbour!

It seems me, Rosie and Her Majesty have unexpectedly come into a fortune, and we have decided, being now three ladies of leisure (as well as three ladies of some considerable means) to visit good old Ameri-kay.

Our ship, The Carpathia, leaves for New York on the next high tide. We might even visit some of Wild Bert's uncles and aunts while we are there, and we will be sure to send back presents to Shep and Calico Tom; and to Madame Flo as well, to thank her for taking the two boys in. Her Majesty is looking forward to chasing some of those big buffalo things that Bert was always going on about!

You know me, I don't like getting mushy.

But I just want to say that I will miss you, dear Bram.

Of all the jewels I have ever seen (and, believe me, I am seeing quite a lot of them now!) you are the shiniest one.

Keep writing, Bram – make a name for yourself, one that I will hear wherever I am in the world. And make me proud.

Your friend,

Mol x

P.S. Be nice to your da–and tell him we say thanks-very-much to him for the you-know-what!

I hope I will meet Molly again, dear Diary.

I hope I will be a writer. I hope I will always remember my adventures in Dublin City.

And I hope I will never forget that I am, and forever will be, a Sackville Street Spook.

Bram

Author's note on Dublin

Many of the Dublin locations in this book are as real as can be and can be visited today. Bram's childhood home at **Marino Crescent** and the little park opposite are still in leafy Clontarf. **Sackville Street** is now called O'Connell Street, and the Dublin Spire now stands in the exact spot where **Nelson's Pillar** once stood. Traders still sell their wares on **Moore Street** and fairs take place at **Smithfield Market** to this day. The U-shaped **Debtors' Prison** stands between Green Street and Halston Street and is sometimes used as a film location for movies. The **Round Room** of the Rotunda Hospital where the great Charles Dickens once performed is still a theatre. The **Phoenix Column** and the beautiful **Dublin Zoological Gardens** can be visited in the Phoenix Park. **Dublin Castle** is still there of course, and the underground **River Poddle** flows beneath it, but the Tavistock Tower where the **Irish Crown Jewels** were held is an invention; the very real Crown Jewels went missing again (in real life this time!) in June 1907. Molly's hut is an invention too, but **Mud Island** is a real place, and the Lock-keeper's Cottage at **Newcomen Bridge** on the Royal Canal still stands. Lastly, **St Michan's Church** near Arran Quay, with its dark crypt full of mummies, is absolutely and terrifyingly real – guided tours are given to children and very brave adults all year round.

Why not visit some of these places the next time you're in Dublin City? They might even inspire you, just like Bram, to become a writer!

The Real Bram & Molly

The real **Bram Stoker** was born and raised in Marino Crescent in Clontarf, in Dublin. After school, he attended Trinity College, Dublin, where he was a star athlete. He always had a great love of writing and theatre.

After college, he first became a newspaper theatre critic, and later a theatre manager in London …and then he decided to combine these two loves to write books such as *Dracula, The Lady in the Shroud*, and *The Lair of the White Worm*. His wife's name was Florence!

Molly Malone is definitely a fictional character, best known from the famous Dublin song of the same name – although many children in Victorian Dublin were forced to live the precarious life of homelessness and hunger that Molly leads in this book. Some children still find themselves living like this today, in Ireland and all over the world. As you go through life, try to think of Molly and the Spooks, the fun they had and the hardships they endured, and remember that a helping hand is always better than a harsh word.

The Song

In Dublin's fair city
Where the girls are so pretty
I first set my eyes on sweet Molly Malone
As she wheeled her wheelbarrow
Through streets broad and narrow
Crying, 'Cockles and mussels, alive, alive, oh!'

She was a fishmonger
And sure 'twas no wonder
For so were her father and mother before
And they both wheeled their barrows
Through streets broad and narrow
Crying, 'Cockles and mussels, alive, alive, oh!'

She died of a fever
And no one could save her
And that was the end of sweet Molly Malone
But her ghost wheels her barrow
Through streets broad and narrow
Crying, 'Cockles and mussels, alive, alive, oh!'

Alive, alive, oh
Alive, alive, oh
Crying, 'Cockles and mussels, alive, alive, oh!'

(Traditional)

Acknowledgements

THANKS to editors Helen Carr and Susan Houlden who never miss a stray comma or a misplaced sock; to Emma Byrne for her brilliant art direction and design; to Sarah Webb for her friendship, advice and encouragement – I tip my safari hat to you, Sarah; to the inestimable Mr Paul Howard; to Nicola Pierce for her book *O'Connell Street – The History and Life of Dublin's Iconic Street* (The O'Brien Press, 2021), which I found to be an invaluable source of information while writing this book, as well as being highly entertaining; to all at The O'Brien Press for being good eggs; and lastly to my family, for putting up with my impromptu Dickens-like dramatic readings of early drafts of the book when they'd clearly much rather have been watching Netflix/Disney+/YouTube, etc.